Meadow United

Alan Wait

Meadow United

Learning Curve Education

First published in the UK in 2014
By Learning Curve Education
148 Muir Wood Road
Edinburgh
EH14 5HQ

ISBN 978-0-9929670-0-0

Prologue

Only one man stood on the deck of the Duchess as she sailed through the darkness that night, early in the summer of 1936. A sliver of moon cast a ghostly light on the black ocean as the rusting steamship made its way slowly towards the west coast of Africa.

Edward Jackson looked over his shoulder to check that he was alone. It was past midnight and the other passengers would be asleep in their bunks.

Reaching into the pocket of his coat, he pulled out a piece of paper and unfolded it carefully. In the pale moonlight it was just possible to make out the lines of a map.

Jackson smiled to himself and whispered a single word.

'Diamonds.'

Chapter 1
MONKEY BUSINESS

Obi the monkey was sitting on his favourite rock. It was late in the afternoon and the meadow was peaceful and still, apart from the occasional sound of parrots squawking deep in the jungle. All over the meadow animals were asleep in the shade of the huge acacia trees.

Sitting near Obi on the branch of a tree was his friend, Chaz the chimpanzee. For the hundredth time, Chaz was explaining why chimpanzees were much more clever than monkeys.

'It's a well known fact that chimpanzees are more intelligent,' said Chaz, who was cleaning his teeth with a stick. 'Even the cleverest monkey in the jungle isn't half as intelligent as a chimpanzee.'

Chaz was Obi's best friend and there was nothing the little monkey enjoyed more than sitting on the rock overlooking the meadow and listening to Chaz.

'What does *intelligent* mean?' Obi asked.

'It means you're smart and that you know lots of useful things,' Chaz explained, pulling himself up the rock with his long arms so that he could sit beside Obi. 'Everyone knows that chimpanzees are the cleverest of all the animals. There isn't anyone on the meadow as clever as me.'

Obi knew it was true. Chaz was smarter than all the

other animals. No matter what question Obi asked, Chaz always knew the answer.

'But why are chimpanzees so clever?'

'Lots of reasons,' said Chaz, 'but mainly because our brains are so large. A monkey's brain is tiny compared to a chimpanzee's.'

'Oh, I didn't know that,' said Obi.

'A chimpanzee's brain is enormous so we can remember a huge number of facts, and that makes us very clever.'

Obi scratched his head. 'I don't think I even know what a fact is.'

'I always forget how dumb monkeys are,' laughed Chaz. 'Monkeys really are the stupidest animals on the meadow.' He shook his head and gave Obi a pitying look, which made the little monkey feel even more worthless.

Obi looked down at his feet. 'I know I'm not intelligent, but I do try to learn new things . . . to become more clever.'

'Clever?' said Chaz, frowning. 'It's just not possible for a monkey to be clever. Monkeys are stupid. A monkey is hardly more intelligent than a banana.'

Obi said nothing. He stared at his feet again and felt foolish. Obi would have given anything to be clever like his friend, but Chaz was right, a chimpanzee was much more intelligent than a monkey could ever be. Sometimes Obi felt ashamed at how little he knew and he wondered why Chaz was happy to have a dim-witted monkey as a friend.

'I know,' cried Chaz in a voice that was so loud that he woke up a hippopotamus that had been snoozing by the lake. 'Why don't we try an experiment?'

'An experiment?' said Obi, looking confused. 'I don't understand.'

Chaz got up and circled Obi. 'An experiment is a kind of test. We can see if it's possible for that monkey brain of yours to learn some facts.' Chaz gave the top of Obi's head a rap with his knuckles.

Obi's face lit up. 'I'd like to try that,' he said, feeling proud to have a friend as clever as Chaz.

The chimpanzee sat down again and folded his arms. 'Hmm . . . let me see,' he said, looking deep in thought. 'All right Obi, here's a simple question . . . of all the animals in the world, which can run the fastest?'

Obi thought as hard as he could. Which animal can run the fastest? That was tricky. He looked at all the animals on the sun-baked meadow below. Herman the hippopotamus was climbing out of the lake and gave a huge yawn as he made his way slowly into the shade. Obi wondered if Herman was the fastest runner.

'Is it a hippopotamus?' Obi asked, hopefully.

Chaz shrieked with laughter and jumped up and down. He laughed so much that he nearly fell off the rock.

'That's exactly the sort of half-witted answer I'd expect from a monkey! How could anyone think a hippo would come first in a running race?'

Obi felt very foolish and wished he knew the answer to Chaz's question. He looked again at the meadow below, but there were so many animals that it was hard to know where to begin. He could see apes, baboons, warthogs, zebras and giraffes. Engelbert, the old elephant, was spraying water from the lake onto his wrinkly face. Obi tried to imagine how fast Engelbert and the other animals could run, but he didn't know the answer to Chaz's question.

'Is it a warthog?' he asked.

'Nope.'

'A gorilla?'

'Wrong again.'

'An elephant?'

'An elephant?' cried Chaz, in disbelief. 'You've got to be joking.'

Obi scratched his head. The experiment wasn't going very well. On the far side of the meadow he noticed Gina the giraffe eating leaves from the highest branches of a eucalyptus tree. Gina looked very peaceful, her big teeth chomping away at the pale green leaves.

'I think I know the answer,' said Obi, his face breaking into a smile. 'It's a giraffe, isn't it? A giraffe is the fastest runner as it has such long legs.'

Chaz shook his head and sighed wearily, which made Obi feel even more stupid. 'The question wasn't which is the *tallest* animal in the world,' he said, in a sarcastic voice. 'It was which animal is the *fastest*. I bet even a monkey could beat a giraffe in a running race.'

Obi finally had to admit that he didn't know the answer.

'It's a cheetah, of course, said Chaz, slapping the top of Obi's head. 'A cheetah is the fastest runner in the animal kingdom and that, my friend, is what is known as a *fact*. Do you think you might be able to store just one little fact in that monkey brain of yours?' Chaz asked, unkindly.

'I don't think I've ever seen a cheetah,' said Obi, with a shrug of his small shoulders.

'And you don't want to either, my friend,' said Chaz, waving a finger in front of Obi's face. 'A cheetah is one of the big cats; not as big as a lion, but it can run like the wind.'

The mention of a lion made the hairs on Obi's tail stand on end. Although he had never seen a lion, Obi knew how dangerous they were as his Uncle Jeffrey had been eaten by a lion. One afternoon during last year's rainy season, Uncle Jeffrey had been sitting on a log, eating a nice banana when suddenly a huge lion with sharp fangs pounced on him and gobbled him up. The memory of what happened to Uncle Jeffrey made Obi shiver.

'A cheetah has a top speed of 70 miles an hour,' Chaz continued, 'which is way faster than a hippo or a giraffe.'

'What does a cheetah look like?'

'Well, I've only seen a cheetah once. As I recall it had a brown coat with big black spots, but I didn't get a proper look at it because I was hiding in a tree. If you had a cheetah on your tail, you'd be in big trouble.'

Obi sat quietly for a moment, trying to imagine what he would do if he ever found himself being chased by a cheetah. Seventy miles an hour sounded very fast. The only way he could escape would be to climb to the top of a tall tree.

'Which is more scary?' Obi asked. 'A cheetah or a lion?'

Chaz's eyes narrowed and his face became serious. 'They're both scary,' he said. 'Very scary indeed, but it's a well-known fact that the lion is the king of the jungle, so a lion is definitely the scariest animal you'd ever meet.'

Obi fell silent again. He tried to imagine what he would do if a lion suddenly appeared when he was sitting on a log, eating a nice banana. Poor Uncle Jeffrey.

'Have you ever seen a lion?' Obi asked, in a quiet voice.

Chaz flicked a large beetle off the rock. It landed on its back, turned over and headed off in the direction of some rotting berries.

'Do you remember that time I went to visit my cousin Raz? It was his birthday and I was taking him a large bunch of bananas as a present.'

'Doesn't Raz live far away in the jungle?'

'Yes. It took me four moons to get there but when I arrived he told me that he didn't want my bananas as all his friends had given him bananas for his birthday and he'd had enough of them. That's gratitude for you. On my way home I stopped at a water hole and nearly jumped out of my skin when I saw some lions.'

'What did they look like?' Even though the idea of meeting a lion was very scary, Obi was fascinated and wanted to know more about lions.

'There's no mistaking a lion. They're enormous brown cats with tufts of hair at the end of their tails, and they've got the sharpest teeth you've ever seen. One bite from a lion would snap you in half. I ran away as fast as my legs could carry me and climbed a tall tree. Lions might be very scary, but they're not very good at climbing trees.'

Obi and Chaz sat quietly for a while. They watched as some of the animals moved slowly across the meadow in the direction of the lake. Obi thought how lucky he was to have a friend as clever as Chaz, but he also wished that he knew some *facts* of his own. Then he wouldn't feel so stupid. But that was the problem – when it came to finding things out, Obi didn't know where to begin.

'I know I'm just a stupid monkey and I'll never be as clever as you . . .'

'Correct,' interrupted Chaz, loudly. 'A chimpanzee is a thousand times more clever than a monkey.'

'But I was hoping you could teach me how to be more intelligent,' continued Obi, shuffling across the rock to sit closer to Chaz. 'If I knew even one or two facts, it would make me much more intelligent.'

'Monkeys just can't learn things,' sniffed Chaz.

'But I've learned that a cheetah is the fastest animal,' said Obi.

'Yes, but do you know which animal is the smallest, or which is the heaviest, or which is the best swimmer, or which has the sharpest teeth?'

Obi shook his head sadly. 'I'd give anything to be more clever,' he said.

'You mean you want to know where facts come from?' Chaz said, folding his long arms.

'Yes I do,' pleaded Obi.

'Facts come from a secret place and hardly anyone knows where it is.'

Obi's eyes nearly popped out of his head with excitement. 'Please tell me. Please Chaz!' he begged.

Chaz looked round to check that none of the other animals were listening. 'All right,' he said in a hushed voice. 'I'll tell you but you must promise to keep it a secret.'

'I promise. I won't say a word to anyone.'

'Very well,' whispered Chaz. 'Facts grow on trees.'

Obi's mouth fell open and he gasped in astonishment. 'Facts grow on trees? Really?'

'Yes they do, but not on the trees that you see around here.' The chimpanzee pointed a long finger at the dark green jungle that surrounded the meadow. 'Facts don't grow on ordinary trees. They grow on a special kind of tree, far away from here, deep in the jungle.'

'What kind of special tree? What does it look like?'

'The Fact Tree is easy to recognize as it's so different from all the other trees in the jungle,' Chaz explained. 'The Fact Tree is bright yellow and is covered from top to bottom in large purple spots.'

'Bright yellow?' repeated Obi. He was very confused. 'I've never seen a yellow tree.'

'Hardly anyone knows about Fact Trees,' said Chaz, 'but I promise you that in the centre of the jungle, there is a large yellow tree with purple spots and it has more facts growing on it than a monkey could ever need. All you have to do is pick the facts from its branches one by one. The more facts you pick, the cleverer you will become.'

'That's amazing!' cried Obi.

'I visit the Fact Tree all the time,' Chaz continued. 'How do you suppose I'm so clever?'

Obi nodded his head in agreement. 'I don't know

anyone who is as clever as you.'

'That's because of the Fact Tree,' said Chaz. The smile on his face stretched from ear to ear. 'Why, just a few moons ago when returning from my cousin's birthday celebrations, I stopped off at the Fact Tree to pick a large bunch of facts.'

'Really?' said Obi. 'You can just pick them from the Fact Tree?'

'That's right,' said Chaz. 'It's just like picking juicy berries. Would you like to learn some of the facts that I picked?'

'Yes please, Chaz. Of course I would! Tell me some facts.'

'Very well,' said Chaz, who was still grinning. 'How about some facts to do with *jumping*?'

'Jumping?' said Obi.

'Yes, jumping. Let me ask you a simple question. If all the animals on this meadow took part in a jumping contest, which do you think would win?'

Obi closed his eyes and thought as hard as he could. This was an even harder question than the last one. He knew all the animals on the meadow, but he couldn't think which one would be best at jumping. Perhaps it was Walter the warthog . . . or Zoe the zebra . . . or maybe Olive the ostrich. Obi was thinking so hard that his head began to hurt.

'Give up?' said Chaz.

'I've no idea what the answer is,' said Obi,

despondently.

'A flea is the best jumper,' declared Chaz. 'A flea can jump over 200 times its own height. If you could jump as well as a flea, Obi, you'd be able to jump over that mpingo tree in one giant leap.'

'Really?' said Obi. He couldn't imagine jumping over even the smallest tree.

'Yes, it's a well known fact,' sighed Chaz, putting on his most intelligent face. 'You're not doing very well with these questions, are you Obi? Maybe I should give you an easier one to try. If a flea would come first in a jumping contest, which animal would come last?'

Obi shook his head. He didn't know the answer to that question either.

'It would be an elephant, of course!' cried Chaz. 'An elephant would always come last at jumping.'

They looked across the meadow to where Engelbert was standing fast asleep. There were lots of fleas buzzing round his huge grey ears and his trunk was curled up.

'No doubt about it,' said Chaz. 'Elephants would definitely come last in a jumping contest.'

'But Engelbert's really old,' Obi pointed out.

'It's nothing to do with age,' said Chaz, shaking his head dismissively. 'An elephant's body is much too heavy and his legs hardly bend at all. No matter how hard an elephant tries to jump, he can't get even the teeniest way off the ground. Yes, my dim-witted little monkey friend, facts are facts. A flea would always come first, and an elephant would always come last.'

Obi looked again at the old elephant snoozing by the edge of the lake. He felt quite sorry for Engelbert. 'Is there any contest that an elephant could win?' Obi asked.

Chaz thought for a moment and nodded. 'Indeed there is,' he said. 'It's a well known fact that of all the animals, an elephant is the best at remembering.'

'Remembering?' said Obi.

'Yes,' said Chaz. 'An elephant never forgets a single thing.'

Chapter 2
NO TIME TO LOSE

After 3 weeks at sea, the Duchess finally reached a small port on the west coast of Africa.

Under the blazing midday sun, the men unloaded the cargo of wooden boxes and crates. Inside were picks and shovels, drills, saws and huge hammers. Others contained hard hats, lamps, buckets, pumps and jigs. The men were miners and they had come to Africa for one reason – to find enough diamonds to make them all fabulously rich.

Their equipment was taken from the port to a nearby railway station where it was loaded onto a freight train. Shrouded in a white plume of steam, the train chugged slowly out of the station, gathering speed as it crossed a wooden bridge, the oily black engine hissing and grumbling as it carried the men and their cargo onwards.

For hundreds of miles the train rumbled across the hot dusty grasslands of the African savannah, passing flocks of coloured birds and herds of animals grazing on tall grasses.

When the railway tracks came to an end and the train could go no further, the men tied the equipment onto the roof of an old yellow bus and, with Jackson behind the wheel, they headed east, deeper into the heart of Africa.

For days the bus crawled along narrow mud tracks baked hard by the fierce sun. They passed huge mountains and crossed dark rivers where lazy crocodiles grinned at them. They went through towns and villages that became smaller and smaller, until there were no more villages and no more people, and the bus could go no further. Ahead of them lay the tallest, darkest, thickest jungle in the whole of Africa.

But the men didn't stop. Picking up the boxes and carrying them on long poles, they set off into the jungle. They made their way slowly through the dense bush, hacking at tangled vines and roots to make a path. The trees grew so high that no sunlight reached the forest floor and it was hard to tell if it was day or night.

But on went the miners, day after day. They trooped along riverbanks, past more crocodiles and enormous snakes, which were wrapped round fallen trees. They trampled over thick carpets of moss and leaves, their boots scattering the spiders, ants and beetles that lived among the plants of the jungle floor. It was hard work. The only sound was the swish of their machetes as they cleared a path, and the screech of birds in the trees around them.

After many days and nights, the explorers emerged from the darkness of the jungle onto a beautiful grassy meadow, which was flooded with glorious yellow sunlight. In the middle of the meadow was a lake with clear blue water and all around were flowers of every possible colour and scent. Huge lizards sunbathed on the rocks and a flock of blue-breasted kingfishers landed softly by the water's edge.

There were animals too – monkeys, apes, baboons, warthogs and lemurs. Hippos and waterbuck grazed side by side on the gently sloping banks of the lake. A mother elephant stood with her calf, watching the explorers as they stumbled wearily out of the jungle, one by one. It was the most beautiful place the men had ever seen.

'This is what we have been searching for!' cried Jackson, pointing towards a hill of purple rocks at the far end of the meadow. 'Over there my friends. That's where we'll find the diamonds. Tomorrow we'll start digging for our treasure!'

The men pitched tents under the shade of umbrella-shaped acacia trees and ate the last of their provisions. They unpacked the equipment and sharpened their tools, getting ready for the next stage of their adventure. Then they wished each other good night and went to sleep under a huge African moon.

Chapter 3
BURIED TREASURE

It took the men two weeks to dig the mine. They smashed rocks with hammers and dug into the hill with their spades and shovels. Deeper and deeper they burrowed, quarrying the rocks and soil until they had tunneled far below the surface of the meadow.

The men who worked inside the mine passed buckets of stones up to the surface where others cracked them open with jack hammers in search of diamonds – diamonds that would make a sparkling necklace for a film star or a glittering ring for the finger of a beautiful princess. Big diamonds, small diamonds ... enough to make each of the men extremely rich.

Although they were a long way from home and they missed their families, the men were happy. At the end of a hard day's work they ate fish from the lake and whatever berries, fruit and nuts they could gather. In the evenings when it was cooler, they played football on the sweet, fragrant grass of the meadow.

The men loved playing football. In one of the crates that they had carried all the way from home was a brown leather football, together with boots, shorts and football shirts – eleven red and eleven blue - with white numbers on the back. There was even a referee's whistle.

The men sawed down trees and used them to make goal posts and crossbars. They sunk the posts into the red soil and hooked up some netting, borrowed from the crates, to catch any balls that flew past the goalkeeper. They marked out the touchlines with small white stones and placed a flag at each corner. The posts and crossbars were painted white and they marked out two penalty spots and a centre circle. When they had finished, it looked just like a proper football pitch.

Every evening the men put on their football boots, shorts and shirts, and played a match. The animals watched from a safe distance, listening to the cries of the players and the thwack of boots on the leather ball as it flew up and down the meadow.

Great shot Vincent!   *Oooh, bad luck James!*
Offside referee!   *Penalty!*

Sometimes a match carried on long after the sun had gone down, the football pitch lit by a huge moon that hung like a lantern in the night sky, flooding the meadow with a banana-coloured glow.

And that was how our band of explorers spent their time on the meadow until the day they discovered the African Queen.

One morning, in the darkest corner of the mine, they unearthed a huge diamond. It was almost as big as the man's fist! When they brought it to the surface everyone came running to stare goggle-eyed at the jewel. For a long time nobody spoke - the men gazed at the diamond, captivated by its beauty.

Eventually, Jackson broke the silence. 'The legend was true,' he said. 'We have found the biggest diamond in Africa.'

'Never mind Africa,' shouted one of the miners. 'It's the biggest diamond in the whole world!'

'It'll be worth a fortune!' cried a third man.

'We'll all be rich!'

'We'll all be millionaires!'

'We'll all be famous!'

Jackson held the diamond above his head and the meadow was suddenly ablaze with all the colours of the rainbow and the lights of a thousand shining stars. It sparkled in the morning sun, reflecting its rays in a magical explosion of colour.

'We must give this diamond a name,' said Jackson. 'What shall we call it?'

'The African Queen,' cried a voice from the crowd.

The others nodded in agreement.

'The African Queen it shall be,' said Jackson, putting the diamond carefully into a leather pouch. 'The African Queen is our destiny, gentlemen. It will bring us fame and fortune. Remember this day. The first of June, nineteen hundred and thirty-six . . . the day the African Queen was discovered. The biggest diamond the world has ever seen.'

'We'd better make sure we don't lose it,' cried one of the miners, and the others laughed.

'Don't worry about that,' said Jackson. 'The African Queen will be kept under lock and key in my tent until we leave the meadow.'

Chapter 4
PENALTY!

The diamond made the men very happy. They shook hands, hugged and slapped each other on the back. They jumped up and down on the dusty red ground, dancing and singing at the tops of their voices.

African Queen ... African Queen!
The biggest diamond the world has seen!

They made such a noise that the animals of the meadow came to investigate. They appeared slowly from every direction and before long, a large crowd had gathered at the edge of the meadow. There were hippos and giraffes, apes and gorillas, elephants, gazelles and impalas, as well as rhinos, warthogs and zebras. Some tiny monkeys and baby chimpanzees pushed their way to the front of the crowd to get a better view.

'Hey, look at all these animals!' shouted one of the men. 'Where have they come from?'

'There are hundreds of them,' cried another.

'What do they want?' asked one of the men nervously.

'Why, they've come to watch us play football,' laughed Jackson. 'Come on gentlemen, let's put on our boots and give our football fans a match to remember!'

Soon the men were running furiously up and down the meadow, playing the best game of their lives, while a large crowd of curious animals watched them.

'Good shot Jack!'

'Brilliant pass!'

'One nil to the Reds!'

'Come on referee ... he was offside a mile!'

Suddenly Jackson cried out in pain and fell to the ground gripping his right leg. The others stopped playing and gathered round him.

'I'm sorry chaps,' groaned Jackson, 'I think the game's over for me. I've twisted my knee.'

'Looks like a bad injury,' said Vincent, the Blue's captain. 'What rotten luck.'

'We should stop the match,' suggested Freddie, the Red's goalkeeper. 'It's bloomin' hot out here.'

'Don't be daft,' said Jackson. 'We've only just started. I'll go and sit in my tent to rest my leg. You men carry on playing.'

Jackson took off his boots and his red football shirt and hobbled painfully towards his tent.

'Are you sure you'll be all right Jackson?' shouted one of the men. 'Shall I come with you?'

'I'll be fine,' said Jackson, giving his knee a rub. 'Anyway,' he said, pointing to the crowd of animals, 'they've come to see you play. You mustn't disappoint your fans.'

And so, with a short blast from the referee's whistle, the match was restarted. The animals watched from a safe distance as the players thumped and thwacked the brown leather ball forwards, backwards, sideways and sometimes so high in the air that it looked just like the midday sun. Their eyes followed the ball from one end of the meadow to the other, and then back again. When the ball flew past the outstretched hand of the goalkeeper and into the net the men cheered loudly.

GOAL!

The longer the game went on, the more excited the animals became. The monkeys started running up and down the touchline, baboons jumped up and down, and chimpanzees screeched so loudly that they startled all the birds on the meadow. Each tackle was greeted by approving grunts from the rhinos and snorts from the warthogs. The baboons barked loudly at every shot, the gorillas grumbled, and the monkeys shrieked with laughter each time the ball bounced off one of the player's heads. After each goal, zebras beat their hooves so hard, that a cloud of red dust rose above the meadow, reaching the long necks of the giraffes, high above the other the animals.

It was a close match. By the time the sun slipped behind the mpingo trees, the Reds and the Blues had each scored nine goals. Then, a sudden blast from the referee's whistle brought the match to a halt.

PENALTY!

The meadow fell silent as the captain of the Blues placed the ball on the penalty spot. In front of him, the Red's keeper stood with a determined look on his face. It was his job to save the penalty kick and stop the Blues winning the match.

The captain took five steps back and wiped the sweat from his forehead. He took a deep breath – just one well-directed shot past the keeper and his team would win the match.

But before he could take the penalty, something very unexpected happened. A baby elephant trotted onto the pitch. He went past the players, with his little trunk curled up in front of him, until he reached the penalty spot. Then, with a swing of his front leg, the little elephant kicked the ball so hard that it flew over the heads of all the men and animals, and disappeared like a speeding cannonball far into the distance. Just when it looked like the ball would disappear, it landed in the highest branches of a huge mpingo tree.

The players stood astonished as the little elephant trotted back to his mother. All the animals watched in silence, waiting to see what would happen next.

One of the men broke the silence.

'Stupid animal!' he shouted, shaking his fist angrily at the baby elephant. 'You've ruined our game!'

'How are we going to get our ball back?' yelled another. 'That must be the highest tree in the whole of Africa. We won't be able to get it down from there.'

'Perhaps the wind will blow it down,' said Freddie.

'No chance,' groaned Stanley. 'It looks well and truly stuck.'

'Maybe Jackson will know what to do,' said Vincent.

'Game's over anyway,' said Charles, untying his football boots. 'Without a ball, I don't suppose we'll be needing these again,' he said angrily, flinging his shirt and boots into a wooden crate.

One by one the men put their shirts, shorts and boots into the crate and the animals began to drift away. Then there was a shout from Jackson's tent.

'Where's Jackson?' cried Vincent. 'He's not in his tent.'

'Maybe he's gone for a walk?'

'How could he go for a walk? He twisted his knee, remember?'

'Wait a minute ... all Jackson's things have gone too,' cried Stanley. 'His boots, his bag and his water bottle.'

The men stood by Jackson's tent looking puzzled, when Vincent suddenly cried out, 'The African Queen! Where's the African Queen?'

'Jackson has the diamond,' shouted one of the men.

'He's taken it!' yelled Bill. 'Jackson's stolen the African Queen!'

Jackson had stolen the diamond and the men were furious. He hadn't been injured at all. He'd been pretending. While the men had carried on playing football, Jackson had sneaked off with the precious diamond.

'Wait til I get my hands on him!' cried Eric.

'He's going to be sorry!' yelled Ted, grabbing a rope.

'After him!' roared Vincent, and the men charged off towards the jungle.

'He's got a start on us but we'll catch him!'

The men burst into the jungle, running as fast as they could. The diamond was missing and they wanted it back. They thrashed through the bushes and leapt over roots and branches, shouting angrily at the tops of their voices.

'We're coming after you Jackson!'

'We know what you've done!'

'You thief!'

'We're going to teach you a lesson!'

But in their anger, the men had rushed into the jungle without any food or water. Worst of all, they had no idea where they were going because Jackson had the only map. It wasn't long before the men became separated, and when the sun went down and darkness descended on the jungle, the men were completely lost. And everyone knows that the jungle is full of man-eating snakes and hungry crocodiles, as well as huge spiders and dangerous swamps.

Chapter 5
AN ELEPHANT NEVER FORGETS

Obi and Chaz were making their way to the lake. It was late afternoon and a gentle breeze rustled in the bamboo growing by the water's edge. Obi skipped along the path with his tail in the air. He and Chaz were on their way to see Engelbert to find out if it was true that an elephant never forgets.

'An elephant is the world's heaviest land mammal,' Chaz explained to Obi. 'Isn't that right, Engelbert?'

The old elephant lifted his long trunk slowly out of the lake and squirted some water into his mouth. 'I guess so,' he said in his deep voice. Then he squirted more water over his back.

'An adult elephant weighs about ten tons,' Chaz continued. 'There's no other animal that's anywhere near as heavy as an elephant.'

'Amazing,' said Obi, looking impressed. He wasn't very good at counting. No matter how hard Obi tried, he could never count past three, but ten tons sounded like a lot.

'I was just telling Obi some facts about elephants,' said Chaz, looking up at Engelbert's craggy face.

'Facts?' said Engelbert.

'Yes, I was explaining that an elephant would come last in a jumping contest.'

'A flea would be the winner,' said Obi, excitedly. 'It's

a well-known fact.'

Engelbert looked doubtful. 'I don't recall ever taking part in a jumping contest.'

'Well, I would advise you not to,' said Chaz, 'because you would come last.'

'I shall try to remember that,' said Engelbert.

'And, I have no doubt that you *shall* remember,' declared Chaz, 'because, as I have explained to Obi, elephants may be hopeless at jumping, but an elephant would definitely win a *memory* contest.'

'A memory contest?' said Engelbert. 'What do you mean?'

'Chaz says an elephant never forgets anything,' said Obi. 'Is it true Engelbert?'

'Go on, ask him to remember something,' said a deep voice from behind them. Herman the hippopotamus had wandered over to join them.

Obi jumped up and down excitedly. 'We should carry out an ex . . . an ex . . . an ex . . .'

'An experiment,' said Chaz, giving Obi an annoyed look. 'That is precisely what I was about to do before you interrupted.'

'Go on then,' grunted Herman. 'What are you waiting for? Ask him a question.'

'You can't just ask *any* old question,' said Chaz. 'A memory experiment has to be handled carefully. Only a chimpanzee is clever enough to carry out a proper test of memory.'

'Chimpanzees are the cleverest animals,' said Obi. 'Chaz's brain is full of facts.'

'Chaz is clever,' Herman agreed. 'A bit too clever for his own good, if you ask me.'

'Well, we don't need your opinion, Herman,' said Chaz, 'because I am about to carry out an experiment which will prove that elephants have the best memories.'

'I can't really see the point of this,' said Engelbert, getting annoyed. 'I was enjoying a nice bath in the lake before you all turned up wanting to ask me questions.'

'Don't worry, Engelbert,' said Obi. 'Chaz knows what he's doing.'

Chaz held up his hands to demand silence. When the animals were quiet, he turned to the elephant. 'Engelbert, can you remember what you ate for lunch on this day five seasons ago?'

Engelbert thought about the question. 'Leaves,' he replied.

'Amazing,' said Obi clapping his hands with excitement. 'I couldn't tell you what I ate for lunch yesterday, never mind five seasons ago.'

'Ask him another question,' grunted Herman the hippo. 'Maybe that was a lucky guess.'

'Very well, I shall try a more difficult one,' said Chaz. 'Engelbert, when was the last time a tree on the meadow caught fire in a storm?'

'Twelve seasons ago,' said Engelbert, without

hesitation. He sprayed more water into his mouth.

'Very impressive,' agreed Herman.

How can you remember things that happened so long ago?' asked Gina the giraffe, who had joined the small group.

'I remember it well,' said Engelbert. 'No rain had fallen on the meadow for many moons and the lake was drying up. Then came the night of the big storm and the sky was on fire with white light. Definitely twelve seasons ago.'

'That proves it!' shouted Obi jumping up and down and clapping his hands. 'It's true. Elephants do have the most amazing memories.'

Obi noticed that they had been joined at the lakeside by more animals of the meadow. Zoe the zebra had arrived and Walter the warthog was making his way over to investigate. Then Misha, another monkey, sat down next to Obi.

'What's all the fuss about?' whispered Misha.

'It's an experiment to show that elephants have the best memories,' explained Obi. 'Engelbert can remember everything that has ever happened on the meadow.'

'How old are you, Engelbert,' asked Gina the giraffe.

The old elephant thought about this for a while. 'Actually, it's my birthday,' he said. 'I believe I am seventy-two seasons old today.'

'That's ancient,' said Zoe the zebra. 'Nobody else

around here is even half as old as you are, Engelbert.'

'You must be older than all the trees in the jungle,' said Walter the warthog.

'I'm not that old!' protested Engelbert.

'What is the furthest back you can remember?' asked Zoe the zebra.

Engelbert closed his eyes for a moment. 'Seventy-two seasons is a very long time. I'll need to think about that.'

The animals waited patiently for the old elephant to speak. A gentle breeze blew across the lake and a parrot squawked somewhere deep in the jungle. More animals were making their way across the meadow to see what was going on. Olive the ostrich waddled across to join the crowd, then Barney and Becky the twin baboons, along with Jengo the gorilla.

Engelbert opened his eyes. 'Well, it was a long time ago but I do remember something very strange that happened when I was a baby elephant.'

'What was that?' Obi asked.

'It was my second birthday and my mother had promised me a party. All my friends were invited and I'd been looking forward to it for ages.'

'I don't see anything strange in that,' said Chaz. 'I always have a party on my birthday and I get lots of presents because I am so popular . . . '

'Be quiet, Chaz!' interrupted Herman. 'We want to hear what Engelbert has to say.'

The animals were silent as the old elephant continued his story. 'I was really looking forward to my birthday party,' said Engelbert, softly, 'but it was spoiled by mankinders.'

'Mankinders!' cried Zoe the zebra. 'Engelbert, are you telling us that there were mankinders here on our meadow?'

'Yes there were,' said Engelbert, 'and they ruined my birthday party.'

'What's a mankinder?' Obi asked.

'That's the name my mother gave to them . . . *mankinders*,' said Engelbert. 'They just appeared from the jungle one day and stayed right here on our meadow.'

'What did the mankinders look like?' said Gina. 'Were they as tall as a giraffe?'

'Did they have huge claws and sharp teeth?' said Obi.

'Were they fierce like lions?' Misha asked.

Engelbert shook his head, flapping his giant ears and sending insects flying in every direction. 'A mankinder looks a bit like an ape or a gorilla. They walk on two legs, but they have odd faces and strange hair on top of their heads.'

'Why did they come to our meadow?' said Walter the Warthog.

'I've no idea why they came, but they spent a lot of time over there,' said Engelbert, uncurling his trunk and pointing it in the direction of the purple hill at the far end of the meadow.

'I don't believe there is any such thing as a mankinder,' declared Chaz, loudly. 'I have certainly never seen one and I suspect Engelbert is just making this up to impress us. If mankinders did exist, I would know at least ten facts about them.'

'Oh, I can assure you that mankinders were here,' Engelbert insisted. 'I may only have been a baby elephant but I clearly remember them climbing that hill over there.'

'Tell us more about the mankinders,' said Misha. 'Did they look like monkeys?'

'They looked pretty strange,' said Engelbert. 'Some mankinders had blue skin and others had red skin. Each night before they went to sleep, they took off their skins and put them in that old crate over there.' The elephant pointed at the dusty wooden crate lying nearby. 'The next day, they opened the crate and put their skins back on. I remember it clearly.'

Obi could hardly believe his ears. 'They took their skins off and put them in a crate?' he cried in amazement. 'How is that possible?'

'It's not true . . .' Chaz began.

'But Engelbert,' said Misha, ignoring the chimpanzee, 'what did the mankinders do to spoil your birthday party?'

A troubled expression spread over Engelbert's

crinkly grey face. 'I remember it was a hot afternoon and I was waiting for my friends to arrive, looking forward to the games we were going to play. But nobody came,' he whispered sadly, moving his trunk slowly from side to side. 'I waited and waited, but not one of my friends arrived.'

'Why?' asked Jengo the gorilla.

'It's rude not to come when you've been invited to a party,' snorted Herman.

'Especially your friends,' added Walter.

'After I'd waited for ages, I decided to look for my friends. It didn't take long to find out why nobody had come to my party.'

'Maybe they'd forgotten,' Obi suggested, helpfully. 'I'm always forgetting things, although I'm sure I'd remember if someone invited me to a party.'

Chaz gave the top of Obi's head a slap. 'The reason you forget things, Obi, is because your monkey brain is too small to remember even the tiniest fact.'

'It was the *mankinders* fault!' roared Engelbert, making all the animals jump. 'They were running around like idiots, chasing a big brown coconut . . . the biggest coconut I've ever seen . . . kicking it from one end of the meadow to the other.'

'Kicking a coconut?' said Walter. 'Why were they doing that?'

'I suspect they'd gone mad,' said Engelbert. 'All my friends were watching the mankinders chase around after the coconut. Every other animal on the meadow was there too, watching their stupid game.'

'That's a shame,' said Obi, who felt sorry for Engelbert.

The elephant nodded. 'I decided that if no one was coming to my party, I was going to have some fun of my own.'

'What did you do?' Misha asked. 'You must tell us, Engelbert.'

Engelbert's face broke into a smile. 'Something happened and the mankinders stopped playing their game. They just stood there staring at the coconut.'

'Then what?' asked Gina, her long eyelashes fluttering with excitement.

'What did you do? Tell us!' cried Barney and Becky the twin baboons.

There was a twinkle in the elephant's eyes. Engelbert was enjoying telling his story. 'I went over to the coconut and I kicked it as hard as I could.'

'Did the coconut smash into pieces?' asked Zoe the zebra.

'That's the strange thing,' said Engelbert, looking puzzled. 'It didn't break at all. It flew up into the sky like a bird. On and on it went, until it got caught in the branches of that big tree over there.'

All the animals stared at the tree on top of the hill. It was the tallest tree on the meadow.

'It was much too high for a mankinder to climb,'

chuckled the elephant. 'Maybe even too high for a monkey like you, Obi.'

'What did the mankinders do?' cried Obi. 'Were they angry when you kicked their coconut into the tree?'

'They were furious,' chortled Engelbert. 'They took off their skins and put them into the crate. Then they went charging off into the jungle, waving their arms and shouting at the tops of their voices. We never saw the mankinders again.'

'Why did they go into the jungle?' asked Obi. 'And why didn't they come back for the coconut?'

Chaz stamped his foot on the ground angrily. 'I have already told you that there were no mankinders here on the meadow. When I said that elephants never forget, I should also have told you that elephants also have the strangest imaginations.'

But Engelbert wasn't listening. He was staring into the distance at the huge mpingo tree. 'Of course, I'm very old now and my eyes might be playing tricks on me, but I'm sure I can still see that coconut up there in the branches of the tree.'

Chapter 6
THE FACT TREE

The evening sun cast ghostly shadows on the rocks, changing their colour from purple to steel grey. The baobab trees stood motionless, their branches etched against the evening sky like huge carrots. As the sun disappeared behind the mountains, the meadow changed colour from green to a shimmering gold, and the last rays of sunlight bathed the meadow in a soft amber light.

Obi and Chaz were sitting on the old wooden crate that Engelbert had spoken about that afternoon.

'Do you think it's true that the mankinders put their skins into this crate?' said Obi.

'Of course it's not true,' snorted Chaz. 'Engelbert is always making up stupid stories. As I told you this afternoon, there is no such thing as a mankinder.'

'Why don't we open the crate and see what's inside?' Obi suggested.

Chaz frowned. 'Forget about mankinders,' he said in a stern voice. 'You shouldn't be so gullible, Obi. You're too quick to believe what others say and one day you'll feel very foolish when someone plays a trick on you. Trust me.'

Obi thought about Engelbert's story. The old elephant seemed quite sure about the mankinders on the meadow all those years ago, and it wasn't like

Engelbert to play tricks on the other animals. But he knew that Chaz was always right.

Obi shrugged and decided to change the subject. 'What about the Fact Tree?' he said. 'I asked Engelbert, but he said he'd never heard of a such a tree.'

'The Fact Tree is real, all right' said Chaz. 'Don't pay the slightest attention to what that elephant says.'

'But how can it be real?' said Obi. 'I've never seen a yellow tree.'

'With purple spots,' Chaz reminded him. 'Listen Obi, you don't have to believe me, but as sure as I'm sitting on this old crate eating palm nuts, the Fact Tree most certainly exists.'

Obi sat quietly. Then, an idea popped into his head and his face lit up. 'Chaz,' he cried, leaping off the crate and jumping up and down with excitement. 'Do you think if I visited the Fact Tree, I could get some facts and become more clever?'

The chimpanzee thought about it. 'Well, you'll never be anywhere near as clever as me,' he sniffed. 'But, yes, I suppose even one visit to the Fact Tree would make you the cleverest monkey on this meadow.'

'Then you must tell me where I can find it!' cried Obi, leaping back onto the crate. 'Where is it, Chaz? How can I find the Fact Tree?'

Chaz grinned. 'You want to find the Fact Tree?'

'Yes, yes, I do!' cried Obi.

'Well, maybe I could help you,' sniffed Chaz. 'But if I

tell you where to find it you must promise to do something for me in return.'

Obi could hardly bear the excitement. 'I'll do anything,' he cried.

'You must promise to bring me thirty bananas every morning for my breakfast.'

The smile disappeared from Obi's face. 'But I can only count to three,' he said, in a soft voice.

'I always forget how hopeless monkeys are at counting,' said Chaz. 'Okay, you must bring me the three largest bunches of bananas you can find. I'm sure even a numbskull monkey like you can manage that.'

'I will,' Obi agreed, his face brightening up immediately. 'Every morning I will bring you the three largest bunches of bananas I can find.'

'Every day . . . for ever and ever.'

'I promise,' said Obi.

'And you must peel each one.'

'I will,' Obi said. 'I will peel every banana.'

'And you must chop them into small pieces to make them easier to eat,' said Chaz.

'I'll do it. I promise,' yelled Obi. The little monkey was almost bursting with excitement. 'And now you have to tell me where I can find the Fact Tree.'

The chimpanzee frowned and looked seriously at Obi. 'To find the Fact Tree you must leave this meadow and go into the jungle. Follow the river upstream for three moons until you reach the centre of the jungle.'

'But how will I know where the centre is?' Obi asked.

'The trees will be so tall that you won't be able to see the sun. You won't hear any birdsong, and the colour of the river will turn from green to black. That's where you'll find the magical Fact Tree.'

'But how will I know which tree it is? There are so many trees in the jungle. How can I be sure which one is the Fact Tree?'

Chaz snorted loudly. 'You'll know it's the Fact Tree, Obi, because even a stupid monkey like you couldn't fail to notice a yellow tree covered in purple spots! As far as I know there's only one Fact Tree in the jungle.'

'But what about the facts?' Obi asked. 'When I find the tree, how will I know what to look for?'

'Easy,' said Chaz, popping a juicy palm nut into his mouth. 'When you find the tree, you'll see that the branches are covered from top to bottom with facts of all shapes and sizes. All you need to do is pick them with your little monkey fingers.'

'Facts really grow on the branches of the tree?' said Obi, looking puzzled. He was finding it hard to imagine what such a tree would look like.

'I admit it's a pretty odd-looking tree,' said Chaz. 'But, I'm telling you the truth Obi. It's covered in facts and all you need to do is pick them.'

'But what do facts look like?' Obi asked.

'Hmmm ... I suppose facts are quite hard to describe if you've never actually seen one,' said Chaz, scratching his chin with his long fingers. 'But there is one sure way to recognise a fact.'

'Tell me,' begged Obi. The excitement was becoming too much for the little monkey. He could hardly wait to go to the jungle to find the magical Fact Tree.

'Well,' said Chaz, the smile on his face growing even wider. 'It's easy to recognise facts because they sparkle and shine.'

'Sparkle and shine?' said Obi. Now he was even more confused. 'What do you mean?'

Chaz looked around to make sure no one was listening. 'Facts come in all different shapes and sizes,' he said in a hushed voice. 'Some are big and some are small, some are thin and some are fat. I've seen round facts and square facts, and once I saw a fact that was shaped almost like a banana. But the one thing they all do is sparkle. Oh yes, my little monkey friend, they sparkle and shine just like the stars above the meadow at night.'

'Amazing!' cried Obi. 'And how many facts should I pick?' he asked. 'I can only count to three.'

Chaz laughed. 'As many as you can hold in your hands,' said the chimpanzee. 'Remember, the more facts you pick, the cleverer you will be. You'd definitely be the cleverest monkey on the meadow, although that's not saying much,' Chaz added with a sniff. 'In my experience, monkeys have always been a bit lacking in the brain department.'

Obi was silent for a moment. He was imagining himself returning to the meadow with his hands full of sparkling, shiny facts. He'd be the cleverest monkey on the meadow.

Obi made up his mind that the next day he would go into the jungle in search of the Fact Tree. He would return a different monkey, a clever monkey, whose brain was full of astonishing, marvelous and fabulous facts. He felt sure that Chaz would be impressed by the new Obi, and proud have him as a friend.

Later that night, Obi sat next to Misha near the top of an acacia tree, curling his tail round a branch. He told Misha all about the magical yellow tree with purple spots whose branches were covered in facts. 'They sparkle and shine just like the stars at night,' he told her. 'I'm leaving as soon as the sun comes up tomorrow to find the Fact Tree and when I come back, I shall be the cleverest monkey on the meadow.'

Misha listened quietly to Obi's plan and when she spoke, she sounded concerned. 'Obi, I know Chaz is your friend, but I hope he's not making fun of you. The jungle is a very dangerous place for a monkey.'

'Chaz would never play a trick like that on me. He's been to the Fact Tree lots of times and that's why he's so clever.'

'I've never heard of a yellow tree with purple spots.

It all seems very strange,' said Misha, doubtfully.

'But it's true,' insisted Obi. 'Chaz has told me where to find the Fact Tree. If I follow the river for three moons I'll reach the exact centre of the jungle, where the trees are so tall that you can't see the sun. There will be no birdsong, and the river will change colour from green to black. That's where I'll find the Fact Tree.'

'Why do you want to be more clever?' said Misha. 'I like you the way you are, Obi.'

Obi sighed and put his chin between his hands. 'I'm fed up being a stupid monkey,' he said softly. 'I'd give anything to be clever like Chaz . . . to know lots of amazing facts. I want to know things that nobody else knows, Misha, and I want to be able to count past three. And most of all, I want all the animals to say, there goes Obi ... the cleverest monkey on the whole meadow!'

The meadow was almost in darkness. The moon and stars were glowing in the night sky, peeking through the treetops and covering the two little monkeys in a silvery light.

'I don't think you should go to the jungle,' said Misha. 'But if you insist on going, I'll come with you.'

Obi shook his head. 'Thanks, Misha, but this is something I need to do on my own. Don't worry though, I'll be careful.'

'Just make sure you stay away from any lions,' said

Misha.

    'I will,' said Obi.

    'And snakes.'

    'I promise.'

    'And crocodiles too.'

    'I'll stay high up in the trees,' said Obi. 'Far away from danger.'

Chapter 7
WHO'S A CLEVER BOY THEN!

The next morning as pale dawn light crept above the slumbering meadow, Obi set off into the jungle. At first he skipped along the riverbank, but soon the paths became tangled with vines and creepers so he climbed up into the trees and leapt from tree to tree. He felt safer in the treetops, away from dangerous snakes and crocodiles.

Although it was tiring, Obi hardly stopped, except to rest a little, or eat a banana. All the time, he could hear Chaz's voice in his head.

'The more facts you pick, the cleverer you will be!'

When night fell on the jungle, Obi found a comfortable spot high up in a mpingo tree where he could curl his tail round one of the branches and go to sleep.

But Obi didn't sleep a wink. There were lots of strange noises in the jungle – the squealing bats flying above his head in the inky black sky, parrots squawking, frogs croaking and the never-ending buzzing of insects. Sometimes he heard animals moving stealthily along the paths below.

And then it began to rain. Obi tried to shelter under some large leaves as the rain beat down on the canopy, turning trickles of water into raging torrents that fell to the jungle floor far below.

When morning finally came, Obi realized that he had never been this far into the jungle. He didn't like being alone, away from his friends on the meadow and he started to feel scared. What if he couldn't find the Fact Tree? What if he got lost and couldn't find his way back to the meadow?

Although Obi was frightened, he tried to be brave and persevere so that he could find the Fact Tree. On he traveled across the treetops, deeper and deeper into the jungle where the vines and creepers grew even more thickly, twisting upwards to find the sun. The river became narrower and darker, its glossy mud banks overgrown with thick ferns and mosses, and Obi could see worker ants carrying rotten fruit and huge spiders spinning their webs.

On the third day of travelling through the jungle Obi realised that he was completely lost. He couldn't see the river any more and all the trees looked the same. There wasn't a yellow tree anywhere to be seen.

Obi sat high in a tree, holding his head in his hands. He was feeling very sorry for himself and ashamed that he would have to return to the meadow and tell Chaz that he had failed in his quest to find the magical Fact Tree. He imagined Chaz laughing at how dumb he had been, rushing off into the jungle like that and getting lost. *What do you expect from a stupid monkey?* Chaz would say. Obi wondered if he'd ever find his way back to the meadow? He might never see

Misha and his friends again, and he began to feel very sad.

Just then, Obi heard a voice.

'Why are you looking so sorry for yourself?' came a loud squawk from the branches above him.

Obi looked round but couldn't see anyone.

'What's the problem mate?' said the voice again.

'Are you talking to me?' asked Obi, softly, peering into the branches.

With a considerable amount of flapping and squawking, a large grey parrot landed on the branch next to him.

'Of course I mean you,' he said, gripping the branch with his sharp talons. 'Who else do you think I'd be talking to? Monkeys don't usually look so miserable. Cheer up for goodness sake.'

'I'm lost,' said Obi, sadly. 'I'm lost and alone in the middle of the jungle and I haven't managed to find the Fact Tree.'

'Fact Tree?' screeched the parrot. 'What Fact Tree? What are you talking about?'

'It's a bright yellow tree with purple spots,' Obi explained, 'It's covered from top to bottom with facts of all shapes and sizes. I've been searching for days, but can't find it anywhere.'

'Yellow tree did you say?' squawked the parrot. 'You don't see many of those in the jungle. My name's Paulie, by the way.'

'I wish I could say I'm pleased to meet you,' said Obi, looking at the ground far below. 'But all I want to do is find my way back to the meadow and see my friends again. It doesn't matter that I'll always be a stupid monkey. I just want to go home.'

'Well,' said Paulie, 'why don't you tell me why you've got yourself lost in the first place. Then we can work out how to get you home.'

Obi told Paulie about the beautiful sunny meadow where he lived and all his friends there. He told him about his best friend, Chaz, who knew all kinds of amazing facts, and how Obi had come to the jungle so that he could be intelligent too. 'But if I can't find the Fact Tree, I'll never be intelligent,' he said, sadly.

When Obi finished his story, the monkey and the parrot sat on the branch deep in thought. Obi watched some blue butterflies dancing in the sunlight and thought how happy they looked.

'Hold on a minute!' screeched Paulie. 'Did you say a yellow tree? How could I forget!' The parrot flapped his wings furiously and his talons gripped the branch even more tightly. 'Why I'm sure I saw a tree like that just this morning, right next to the pond where I had my breakfast.'

Obi could scarcely believe his ears. 'Was it the same colour as a banana?' he cried.

'Yes, it was . . . exactly the colour of a banana,' squawked Paulie. 'I remember thinking to myself that it was very strange to see a yellow tree, covered in purple spots.'

'Purple spots!' yelled Obi, his eyes wide in astonishment. 'Was it covered from top to bottom with sparkling facts?'

The parrot cocked his head to the side. 'I was eating breakfast at the time, so I didn't pay it much attention. Perhaps there were things on the branches but I can't say for sure. My memory isn't what it used to be,' added the parrot with a squawk.

'It has to be the Fact Tree!' shouted Obi, his heart filling with hope. 'Where is it?' he cried, jumping up and down on the branch. 'Can you show me where it is Paulie?'

'I can take you there but we'll have to be very careful as it's dangerous by the pond. We'll need to keep our eyes and ears open.'

Paulie flew along the narrow path while Obi followed, skipping over tangled vines and tree roots as fast as his little arms and legs would carry him.

'This way,' squawked the parrot. 'Follow Paulie .... Not far now ...... Follow Paulie .... Who's a clever boy then!

Chapter 8
THE PRISONER

Obi and Paulie found themselves at a bend in the river, where the trees were so tall and dense they could no longer see the sun. The colour of the river had changed from green to inky black and the jungle was silent. There were no birds singing in the trees, no insects buzzing and nothing moved. Everything was completely still.

This has to be the place, Obi thought, as he looked round at the dark glade. It's just the way Chaz described it.

'Over there, Obi,' squawked Paulie. 'Isn't that the tree you're looking for?'

Obi stood in astonishment with his mouth wide open. There, by the edge of the river, was a yellow tree with large purple spots. 'It's true,' Obi gasped. He had almost given up hope of finding the Fact Tree, and there it was, right in front of his eyes.

'I knew I'd seen a yellow tree somewhere,' cried Paulie. 'What a strange looking tree it is. Come on, let's take a closer look.'

'But where are the facts?' Obi said. 'Chaz said the branches would be covered with facts, but I can't see any. Just plain leaves like any other tree.'

Obi was confused. He had found the Fact Tree, but he couldn't see any facts hanging on its branches. He noticed something lying at the bottom of the tree and he picked it up. 'I wonder what this is?'

'It's a boot,' squawked the parrot.

'A boot?' Obi repeated. 'What's that?'

'A mankinder's boot,' said Paulie. 'Mankinders wear them on their feet. This one looks very old.'

'Mankinders,' said Obi, in a quiet voice. He recalled Engelbert's story about the strange mankinders who had visited the meadow many years before.

'And this ...' declared Paulie, 'unless I'm mistaken ... is a hat.' Paulie pecked at the tattered old hat with his sharp beak. A large spider with furry legs appeared from under the brim and scuttled away into the undergrowth. 'Mankinders put them on their heads.'

Obi sat down and scratched his head. Now he was even more confused. He had come all this way in search of facts and all he'd found was mankinder belongings. 'How do you know about mankinders Paulie?' he asked. 'My friend Chaz says there are no such things as mankinders.'

'Mankinders!' screeched Paulie. 'Don't talk to me about mankinders.' The parrot flapped his wings furiously. 'I don't care if I never see another mankinder as long as I live!'

'You've actually *seen* a mankinder?' gasped Obi. 'In the jungle?'

'No, not in the jungle,' squawked Paulie. 'In a mankinder house.'

'What's that?'

'Oooh, I told you not to get me started about mankinders,' hooted Paulie, his wings flapping in a blur of grey feathers. 'It was a mankinder house in a place called London.'

'London,' repeated Obi. 'I have never heard of that. Is it far from here?'

'Yes, a very long way away,' squawked Paulie. 'I'm not sure I want to talk about it. I still have nightmares about that house and the cage where I was kept,' he added with a shiver.

'My friend Engelbert says that mankinders walk on two legs and they take their skins off each night and put it in a crate. Is that true, Paulie?'

Paulie cocked his head and closed one eye while he thought about Obi's question. 'Well, it's true that mankinders walk on two legs,' he said. 'But I couldn't say what they do with their skin at night. I hardly ever saw what mankinders did because I was trapped in a horrible bird cage for five years.'

'Why were you there?' asked Obi. 'Did you want to go to London?'

'What?' screeched Paulie. 'You think I wanted to spend all that time squashed in a cruel cage for five whole seasons with nothing for company but a little mirror, a perch to sit on and a few mouldy old seeds? Oh no,' screeched Paulie, 'it was a bloomin' nightmare .... a nightmare I tell you ...'

'But why were you there?' Obi asked. 'What happened?'

'It's a long story,' said Paulie, hopping onto the branch of a nearby tree. 'Many moons ago, I was a young parrot growing up right here in the jungle. I was as happy as a parrot could be, going where I pleased, eating seeds and berries, or sometimes a nice piece of fruit. I didn't have a care in the world. One day I was sitting on a tree not far from here, just minding my own business and thinking about what I might like for lunch, when the next thing this bloomin' great net was thrown over me and I couldn't get out. I was trapped.'

'Trapped in a net,' cried Obi. 'Who did that to you?'

'Mankinders of course!' screeched Paulie. 'They caught me and squashed me into a box. Then they took me on a long journey. I lost count of the number of moons I was kept in the box, but it seemed like forever. Just when I had given up hope of ever seeing daylight again, the box was opened and I found myself in a pet shop.'

'What's a pet shop?' said Obi, scratching his head.

'It's a place where mankinders keep animals locked up in cages. Not just parrots, there were all kinds of animals. There was a little furry animal called a mouse and a strange looking creature called a tortoise. In the cage next to me was a guinea pig, and next to him was a rabbit with long pink ears; his name was Gerald. There was even a baby monkey in one cage.'

'A monkey,' gasped Obi. The thought of being captured by mankinders and kept prisoner in a cage for a long time made the hairs on the back of his neck stand on end. He didn't like the sound of the pet shop one bit.

'One day a mankinder came into the shop,' Paulie continued. 'I didn't like the look of him at all. He walked round the shop poking his big hairy face at each cage, wiggling his fat fingers and scaring the living daylights out of all the animals. He stopped at my cage and asked the owner of the shop what kind of bird I was. The owner told him I was an African grey parrot, and that African greys are extremely good at copying the way mankinders speak. *"How much for the parrot?"* he asked. *"He's yours for twenty quid mate."* And that is the story of how I came to be trapped in a cage in the big hairy mankinder's house in a faraway place called London.'

Obi could scarcely believe his ears. 'What was it like living with the mankinder?' he asked. 'Was he friendly ... was he kind to you?'

The parrot gave a loud squawk and flapped his wings again. 'I think most of the time he just forgot about me. He used to lie there on the sofa all day watching TV.'

'TV,' said Obi, with a puzzled expression. 'I don't think I've heard of TV.'

'Well, that's not surprising. You don't see TVs in the

jungle,' said Paulie. 'But watching TV was just about all that hairy idiot ever did. *Match of the Day* ... *Coronation Street* ..... *X Factor* . ... it was a nightmare! Sometimes he didn't even bother to turn it off when he went to bed, which meant I hardly got any sleep.'

'I don't understand,' said Obi. 'Why did he want you to live in his house? Did he want you to be his friend?'

'At first he did,' croaked Paulie. 'Every day he stuck his big hairy face in front of my cage and said, "*Who's a clever boy then? Who's a clever boy?*" trying to get me to speak like a mankinder. Parrots are very good at copying mankinder words and I could have done it easily, but as he kept me locked up in a cage, I decided that I wasn't going to speak for him. Not a single word.'

Obi felt sorry for Paulie. Shut in a cage all day and being forced to speak like a mankinder seemed very unfair.

'He was driving me crazy,' cried Paulie. 'So, one morning when he was standing there saying, "*Who's a clever boy then?*" and poking his fat finger into the cage, I decided I'd had enough, and I nipped his finger as hard as I could with my beak.'

Obi looked at Paulie in amazement. 'You bit the mankinder's finger?' he said. 'Did it make him angry?'

'Oh yes,' squawked Paulie. 'He was angry all right. He danced around the room holding his finger, stamping his big feet on the floor and shouting at the top of his voice. I wouldn't like to repeat some of the words he shouted at me, although I could very easily because African greys are very clever at copying mankinder speak.'

'So what did he do?'

'He gave up trying to teach me to speak like a mankinder. The next day, he went back to the pet shop and came home with a hamster called Marvin and he soon forgot about me.'

The parrot looked down at the ground and shook his head sadly. 'And that was my life for five whole seasons. Trapped in a cage, with nothing to do except watch stupid TV programmes all day and night. It was bloomin' torture.'

Obi climbed onto the branch and sat down beside Paulie. 'How did you get back to the jungle?' he asked. 'Did the mankinder set you free?'

'Oh, no, there is no way the mankinder was ever going to do that,' said Paulie. 'But one day he forgot to shut the door of my cage,' said Paulie. 'I knew it was my one chance to escape so, the moment he left the room to put the kettle on, I jumped out of the cage and flew out of the house through an open window.'

'You escaped!' cried Obi.

'I was free!' cried Paulie. 'I headed south as fast as my wings would carry me. I flew over towns and villages, farms, rivers and the deep grey ocean. I flew day and night, barely stopping at all. Then, just when I thought my wings would carry me no further, I saw the blue mountains of my homeland and the jungle where I had grown up all those seasons ago.'

When Paulie finished his story, the monkey and the parrot sat quietly for a while. Obi looked up at the Fact Tree and wondered what he should do next. Then he heard another voice.

Chapter 9
THE ARGUMENT

'What a tragic story,' said the deep, gravelly voice which came from the river.

Obi climbed down from the tree and peered into the murky water where he saw a huge crocodile with a pointed snout and pale green eyes on top of its flat head. When the crocodile opened its huge jaws Obi could see rows of sharp teeth and he quickly jumped back from the riverbank. He knew how dangerous crocodiles could be.

'I couldn't help overhearing your friend. A sad story always brings a tear to my eye,' said the crocodile in a very polite voice. 'The name's Carl, by the way.'

'Well, it's none of your business, anyway,' squawked Paulie, from the safety of the Fact Tree. 'Don't you know it's rude to listen to private conversations?'

Obi watched the crocodile glide silently through the water towards him. No wonder crocodiles could be so dangerous, they'd be upon you before you realised they were there.

'A thousand apologies, dear friend,' said Carl. 'I rarely get the chance to enjoy company and it can get very lonely in this little glade. Apart from myself and Sigmund, hardly anyone ventures this deep into the jungle.'

The monkey and the parrot looked at each other. 'Who's Sigmund?' they asked at the same time.

'I am Sigmund,' came a voice, not from the river this time, but from somewhere above them. Obi peered into the thick green leaves and tangled creepers above his head. "Who's there?' he asked.

'I'm trying to get some sleep,' said the voice, sounding quite annoyed. 'Go somewhere else to have your conversation and leave me in peace. It's time for my afternoon snooze.'

'Sigmund,' said Carl, 'there is no need to be so rude to our visitors. Why don't you come down and introduce yourself.'

'I hardly got a wink of sleep last night,' came the voice again. 'I'm not getting any younger you know, and I need my beauty sleep.'

'It's the tree,' gasped Obi, pointing at the yellow tree in front of them. 'The Fact Tree is speaking to us.'

'Impossible!' shrieked Paulie. 'Never in all my days in the jungle have I heard a tree speak.'

'But that's where the voice is coming from,' cried Obi. With his tail in the air he got to his feet and scrambled over the roots and creepers until he was standing right in front of the Fact Tree. 'Are you the Fact Tree that my friend Chaz spoke about?' asked the monkey.

'Why, that's not a tree,' cackled Carl, with a huge toothy grin. 'That's Sigmund!'

'But, it must be the Fact Tree,' cried Obi. 'It's exactly as my friend Chaz described. A yellow tree with purple spots.'

'I think you must be mistaken,' chuckled the crocodile, climbing out of the river and settling down on the riverbank. 'There is no such thing as a talking tree. Sigmund, why don't you come down and say hello to our new friends.'

'Oh, alright. I'm not going to get much peace around here, am I?'

Slowly the tree started to move. Obi watched in amazement as the purple spots danced in front of his eyes. The yellow trunk was moving too, uncoiling and slithering in circles, round and round, lower and lower, until a scaly yellow head appeared from behind one of the branches.

Obi rubbed his eyes to make sure he wasn't imagining it. There, in front of him, wasn't a tree at all, but the biggest snake he'd ever seen, and its bright yellow skin was covered in large purple spots. 'You're … a … a … a … snake!' he stuttered.

'Snake! Snake!' screeched Paulie, flapping his wings furiously.

'The name's Sssssigmund, actually,' hissed the snake, his forked tongue flicking in and out of his mouth. 'And I'd appreciate it if you could keep the noise down.'

'For some reason Sigmund, our visitors seem to

think that you are a talking tree,' chuckled Carl, his long tail smacking up and down on the riverbank.

Obi sat down on a log, holding his sad face between his hands. Now he was feeling even more foolish. He had come all this way into the jungle in search of the magical Fact Tree, and all he'd found was a sleepy python and some old mankinder belongings. The little monkey's eyes started to fill with tears.

'Why are you so sad?' asked Sigmund. 'And what's all this nonsense about a talking tree?'

Obi wiped away a tear and took a deep breath. He told Sigmund and Carl all about his journey into the jungle and his dream of being clever. He also explained how he had followed Chaz's directions to find the Fact Tree.

'I wanted to show everyone on the meadow that I'm not a stupid monkey, but I haven't managed to find any facts, not one. And, to top it all, I'm completely lost and don't know if I can find my way home.'

The others were quiet for a moment, until Sigmund spoke. 'I think Chaz has played a nasty trick on you. I very much doubt that the Fact Tree exists. It sounds to me that your friend made the whole story up.'

Obi shook his head. 'Chaz would never play a trick on me. He's my best friend and he's the cleverest animal on the meadow. The Fact Tree must be somewhere in the jungle and I'm going to keep looking for it so that I can get some facts.'

'You shouldn't get upset because of some stupid tree,' said Carl. 'If it's facts that you're after, you've come to the right place. Open your ears my little friend and I will amaze you with some fascinating facts about crocodiles.'

'Hold on a minute,' interrupted Sigmund. 'Why would anyone want to know about crocodiles? They are unquestionably the dullest, most boring creatures in the whole jungle. All crocodiles do is lie around in muddy rivers. Snakes are much more interesting. Listen to my astonishing facts about sssssnakes.'

'What rubbish!' cried Carl, snapping his jaws together fiercely and shaking his tail from side to side. He clambered up the riverbank and moved closer to Obi. 'A crocodile is ten times more interesting than a snake. Fact number one - crocodiles have existed for two hundred and forty million years,' declared Carl proudly. 'Our ancestors lived on the earth at the same time as the dinosaurs. We are much, much older than snakes.'

'I believe you are mistaken' hissed Sigmund. 'Snakes have been around far longer than that. It was a snake that got Adam and Eve into trouble,' said Sigmund, flicking his tongue from side to side. 'That's much more impressive don't you think?'

'It's not the least bit impressive,' snapped Carl. 'All that proves is that snakes cannot be trusted. Why should anyone believe what a snake has to say?'

'You can't argue with the facts,' hissed Sigmund. 'Besides, snakes are much more interesting than crocodiles. Fact number two - there is only one kind of crocodile, but there are lots and lots of different snakes. There are pythons like me, of course, but there are also mambas, cobras, copperheads, vipers, rattlesnakes and sea snakes. There are over two thousand types of snake, but just one plain, boring old crocodile.'

'A trivial detail,' said the crocodile, snootily. 'There may be many types of snake, but there has never been a snake as large as a crocodile. A crocodile is the world's largest reptile, much larger than any snake.'

'Larger, maybe,' hissed Sigmund, 'but not longer. Pythons can grow up to forty feet long, much longer than any crocodile.'

'A crocodile has the sharpest teeth,' declared Carl, opening his powerful jaws wide to prove his point. 'What have you got to say about that?'

'That's nothing!' cried Sigmund. 'Some snakes have more than 200 teeth.'

'But who are the better swimmers?' argued Carl. 'Crocodiles have a top speed of 25 miles an hour.'

'Perhaps so,' hissed Sigmund. 'But snakes are much better at climbing. I'd like to see a crocodile try to climb a tree.'

'Crocodiles can stay under water for up to three hours. I'd like to see a snake try that!'

'Snakes can change their skin six times a year. I'd like to see a crocodile do that!'

'Crocodiles can see in the dark.'

'Snakes can go a whole year without eating.'

'Stop!' yelled Obi at the top of his voice. His head was spinning and he needed to sit down. 'I'll never be able to remember all this,' he cried. 'My brain just isn't big enough to hold all these facts.'

'Well, he started it,' said Carl.

'No I didn't,' hissed Sigmund.

'Why don't you both be quiet,' squawked Paulie. 'Parrots are much more interesting than snakes or crocodiles. Let me tell you some fascinating facts about parrots.'

But Obi had stopped listening to them because something else had caught his attention. A strange object was dangling from a branch at the bottom of the tree, near the tattered mankinder boots. He looked closer and saw that it was a brown leather pouch.

'What have you got there?' asked the snake.

'Looks like one of the mankinder things,' said the crocodile.

'I suspect the mankinder who wore those boots suffered a most unfortunate fate,' said Sigmund.'

'He was probably snapped in half by a fierce crocodile,' declared Carl.

'More likely crushed by a giant python and swallowed whole,' hissed Sigmund.

Obi opened the pouch and peered inside.

'What is it?' asked Paulie.

Obi removed the diamond from the pouch and held it up above his head. The jungle was suddenly glowing with all the colours of the rainbow. The jewel lit up the little glade in an explosion of purples, greens, blues and reds.

'Awesome,' said the crocodile, the dazzling colours reflecting in his eyes like Christmas tree lights.

'It must be a sunbeam,' said Sigmund, 'or a rainbow.'

Obi returned the stone to its pouch and fastened it tightly, then hung it securely by a cord round his neck. It wasn't a sunbeam or a rainbow. Obi knew exactly what it was. It was the biggest, shiniest fact in the whole world.

'Come on Paulie,' he said. 'It's time for me to go home. Let's go back to the meadow.'

Chapter 10
SEARCH PARTY

The rain finally stopped and the sun came out from behind the clouds, bathing the meadow in a soft, straw coloured light. Steam was rising from the rainwater pools that had collected among the rocks. In the distance a giant kingfisher hovered above the lake for a moment, before plunging like a feathered harpoon to spear a fish with its long sharp beak.

A family of baboons sat quietly in a sunny spot, while a shy gazelle emerged from the tall grassy shrubs and strolled towards the lake. As the last remaining drops of rainwater evaporated into the mid-morning haze, the honeybees returned to their business of gathering pollen from the brightly coloured flowers scattered around the meadow.

A group of animals had gathered at one end of the meadow, beside the old football goals. A few flecks of white paint remained on the wooden posts and the rickety crossbar.

'Obi's been missing for six moons,' Misha said to the others. 'I'm worried that something terrible has happened to him.'

Chaz, Engelbert, Herman, Zoe and Walter were all concerned. Barney and Becky the twin baboons came over to join them, along with Gina the giraffe and Jengo the gorilla.

'Obi has never gone off like this before,' said Becky.

'I hope he's alright,' said Barney.

'Should we send out a search party?' suggested Herman. 'He might be in trouble.'

Misha turned to Chaz who was leaning against one of the goal posts cleaning his teeth. 'You must know where Obi is,' she said. 'It was you who encouraged him to go to the jungle.'

Chaz scratched the top of his head. 'I haven't a clue where the dim-witted monkey is. The last thing I heard was that he was going to look for something.'

'What was he was looking for?' asked Gina the giraffe.

'Who knows,' said Chaz. 'I've told him lots of times that the jungle is a dangerous place to go exploring alone. If he's been eaten by a crocodile then it serves him right for not listening to my advice.'

'That's not very nice,' said Zoe the zebra. 'I thought Obi was your friend. Wouldn't you be sad if he was eaten by a crocodile?'

Chaz climbed up onto the crossbar. 'Of course I'd be sad,' he said, looking down at the other animals. 'But if Obi is foolish enough to go to the jungle by himself, it just proves how stupid monkeys are. If he's got himself into trouble, then it's his own fault.'

'Not everyone's as clever as you are,' said Misha. 'And I don't think it's fair to call Obi stupid. If he went to the jungle on his own, he must have had good reason. I'm sure he said it had something to do with a magical tree.'

'A magical tree?' snorted Chaz. 'I've never heard such nonsense.'

'A Fact Tree, I think he called it,' said Misha.

'Why would Obi go off to look for a tree?' asked Gina.

Chaz sighed. 'Who can say what was going on in that tiny monkey brain,' said the chimpanzee. 'We'll probably never know. He's been gone six whole moons, so I doubt we'll ever see Obi again.'

'I'll miss him,' said Becky.

'Me too,' said Barney.

'Obi should have stayed here on the meadow where it is safe,' said Jengo, nodding wisely.

'We can't just give up on him,' cried Misha. 'What if Obi's lost in the jungle and needs our help? We must organise a search party to find him.'

At that moment, a figure emerged from the jungle, skipping across the meadow on all fours. It was Obi and flying above his head was a large grey parrot.

'Obi?' gasped Misha.

'Hey guys,' yelled Obi at the top of his voice. 'I'm back! It's great to see you all!'

'It is Obi!' shouted Engelbert.

The little monkey was back among his friends and he wanted to them all about his adventure.

'There I was lost in the jungle, searching for the

Fact Tree,' he began. 'I'd given up all hope of ever finding it when I met my new friend Paulie . . . hey, this is Paulie the parrot by the way.'

'Pleased to met you all,' squawked Paulie.

Obi jumped onto the old crate and continued his story. 'Luckily for me, Paulie had noticed the yellow and purple spotted Fact Tree that very morning and he showed me where to find it, although it turned out that it wasn't a yellow tree after all, but a huge snake that was wrapped round a tree, and then the snake and the crocodile had a big argument about who was more interesting . . .'

The animals stared at Obi. They were glad to see him back safely, but he didn't seem to be making much sense.

Chaz jumped down from the crossbar and jabbed a finger on Obi's chest. 'Have you gone completely mad?' he cried. 'I've never heard anything so ridiculous in my life.'

'But it's true,' cried Obi. 'I'm not making this up, am I Paulie?' he said turning to the parrot.

'Well ...' began Paulie.

'Never mind,' said Misha, interrupting Paulie. 'We're just glad that you're back safe and well. We were scared you were lost and that we might never see you again.'

'We thought you'd been eaten by a crocodile,' said

Barney.

'Or swallowed by a lion,' added Becky.

Obi looked at his friends and realised how much he had missed them. He'd missed the meadow too. This was his home, and it was where he belonged.

'I'm sorry you were all worried about me,' said Obi. 'I only went to the jungle to find the Fact Tree. Chaz told me that the Fact Tree would make me more intelligent.'

'I said no such thing!' spluttered Chaz. 'You didn't go to the jungle at all,' he snapped, pointing an accusing finger at Obi. 'You were just hiding in those bushes over there, pretending that you were in the jungle. It's just like a pea-brained monkey to play a stupid trick, making us worry that something had happened to you.'

'I don't remember you being the least bit worried,' said Misha, looking sternly at Chaz. 'You said if Obi had been eaten by a crocodile it would serve him right.'

'That's a lie,' yelled Chaz angrily. 'Obi is my friend and I would be terribly upset if anything happened to him. I just got annoyed because he played a silly trick on us, pretending that he was off having an adventure in the jungle.'

'But it's true,' cried Obi. 'I can prove it . . . let me show you what I brought back from my adventure.' The little monkey's fingers loosened the ties of the leather pouch round his neck. 'Maybe you'll believe me when you see this . . .'

But just as Obi reached into the pouch, an enormous roar made all the animals jump. A huge cat had suddenly appeared from the tall grasses and was running towards them at full speed.

'Lion!' screamed Zoe. 'Let's get out of here!'

Chapter 11

THE BIG CATS

The terrified animals ran as fast as they could but more lions surrounded the meadow.

'We're done for!' shrieked Herman.

'Every chimp for himself,' squealed Chaz, knocking Misha over in his rush to escape.

There weren't just lions, there were cheetahs and leopards too, and no matter which way they turned, a big cat was blocking their path. Only Paulie managed to escape by flying to safety high up in a nearby tree.

Suddenly the biggest lion roared, 'Stop!' and all the animals froze. They huddled together in a quivering group, their hearts racing and their eyes wide with fear, waiting to see who would be first to disappear into the lion's mouth.

'Please don't eat me!' shrieked Chaz, who was closest to the lion. He shoved Obi so hard that the little monkey was catapulted forward and landed at the lion's feet. 'Monkeys are much more tasty,' Chaz added.

The lion looked at the animals. He sniffed the air, his grey beard blowing gently in the soft breeze. His tail moved from side to side in a slow steady rhythm, swatting the flies and mosquitoes. He moved closer to the terrified animals and when he spoke they could see his razor-sharp fangs.

'If you all do exactly as I say, nobody will be eaten.'

A smile spread slowly across the lion's face. 'But, how rude of me,' he said, 'I haven't introduced myself. My name is Lionel, but everyone calls me Boss. Isn't that right boys?'

'Yes, Boss,' cried all the cats together.

'Let me introduce you to some of my friends,' said Boss, waving a huge paw in their direction. 'This fine-looking lion behind me is Rio. Say hello to the animals, Rio.'

'I'm starving, Boss,' growled Rio. 'What about my lunch? That zebra over there looks very tasty.'

'You're always starving Rio,' said Boss. 'But I have given these animals my word that they will come to no harm if they do as I say.'

'Yes Boss,' muttered Rio, keeping his eyes fixed on Zoe the zebra.

Boss continued his introductions. 'These two lions are Ralph and Tickles ...'

'Tickles!' Obi whispered to Misha. 'What kind of name is that for a lion?'

'He's not as scary as that one over there,' whispered Misha, pointing to a huge one-eyed lion who had a deep scar that ran all the way down his face.'

'I see you've noticed Scarface,' said Boss. 'After me, Scarface is the most fearsome lion in the jungle. Why don't you introduce yourself to our new friends?'

The one-eyed lion stepped forward and surveyed the

frightened animals. Then he let out a terrifying snarl that made Obi and the others jump.

'I bet he was the lion that ate Uncle Jeffrey,' said Obi.

'Shhhh . . .' whispered Misha, putting her hand over Obi's mouth. 'We don't want to make them angry.'

A smaller cat with a brown coat and black spots stepped forward. 'And this is Zeff,' said Boss.

'That must be a cheetah,' whispered Obi. 'I'm sure Chaz said that a cheetah has black spots.'

'Zeff is the fastest animal in the whole jungle,' continued Boss. 'He has a top speed of one hundred miles an hour.'

'Seventy,' said Obi, in a small voice, but loud enough for Boss to hear.

Boss fixed his eyes on Obi. 'Did you say something, monkey?' he growled.

Obi stared at the ground, wishing that a big hole would open and swallow him up before Boss did. His mouth was dry and his legs were shaking. Although Obi was more frightened that he had ever been in his life, something gave him the courage to speak.

'It's *seventy* miles an hour,' he said in a tiny voice.

'What do you mean, seventy?' demanded Boss.

'A cheetah has a top speed of seventy miles an hour, not a hundred.'

For a moment Boss stood perfectly still. His eyes narrowed as he glowered at Obi and no one dared to move. Obi could hear his heart thumping loudly in his chest. Then Boss roared with laughter. 'How can a monkey possibly know how fast a cheetah can run? Have you ever seen a cheetah run?'

'No,' replied Obi, timidly.

'Then why are you contradicting me?' said Boss. 'If I say a cheetah has a top speed of one hundred miles an hour, then that is exactly how fast Zeff runs. Isn't that right, Zeff?'

'That's right, Boss,' hissed the cheetah. 'Hundred miles an hour . . . easy.'

Obi swallowed hard. 'My friend Chaz told me that a cheetah has a top speed of seventy miles an hour. It's a well-known fact.'

'A fact?' said Boss. 'What do you mean a fact? What are you gibbering about?'

'Shut up, Obi,' hissed Chaz, who was hiding behind Herman the hippo. 'You're going to get me into trouble.'

'Enough of this nonsense!' roared Boss. 'Okay boys, tell them who we are.'

'We're the Big Cats!' cried the lions, cheetahs and leopards.

'That's right, the Big Cats,' said Boss. 'Nice place you've got here,' he added, looking approvingly around the meadow. 'Wouldn't you agree, gentlemen?'

'Very nice, Boss,' echoed the Big Cats.

Boss turned his attention back to Obi and his friends. 'The Big Cats have been looking for a place to spend the rainy season and I think we have just found the perfect spot, right here on this meadow. What do you say boys?'

'Yes, Boss,' cried the Big Cats.

'That's decided then,' declared Boss. 'Tomorrow the Big Cats will move in, and you lot,' he said, waving his paw at the animals, 'will be moving out!'

The animals looked at each other, too frightened to speak or move.

'There's no reason for any of you to be afraid,' said Boss, smiling. 'We're not going to be unreasonable about this, are we boys?'

'No, Boss,' cried the Big Cats.

'As long as you leave before the sun goes down, you will come to no harm.'

Then his eyes narrowed, he bared his teeth and his smile was replaced by a dark, threatening scowl. 'But I warn you,' he said, 'we will return at sunrise with lots of Big Cats and any of you foolish enough to stay on the meadow will be eaten for breakfast.'

A friendly smile returned to Boss's face. 'I'd say we're being very reasonable.'

'Very reasonable, Boss,' agreed the Big Cats.

While the animals stood confused and frightened, Obi held his head high. Although he was scared, he couldn't allow the Big Cats to take over the meadow without speaking up. The meadow was their home and it wasn't fair to make them leave. Someone had to stand up to Boss and the Big Cats.

'Excuse me, Boss ....' began Obi, in a small voice.

'What is it?' growled the lion.

Obi took a deep breath. His mouth was dry and his hands were trembling, but he went on. 'The Big Cats are very welcome to live here on the meadow,' he said in a small but steady voice, 'but it isn't fair that we have to leave. There's plenty of room for us all here and this is our home. Perhaps we can be friends and share the meadow?'

Boss stared at Obi as if he couldn't believe his ears.

'Share?' he roared. 'Did I just hear a monkey tell me that the Big Cats must *share* this meadow?' Boss bared his teeth and thrust his nose so close to Obi's face that the little monkey could feel the lion's whiskers against his cheeks. 'I've a good mind to teach you a lesson,' roared the lion. 'I should eat you up right now!'

'Take it easy, Boss,' cried one of the lions.

'Count to ten, Boss,' advised one of the leopards.

'Remember your blood pressure,' said a cheetah.

Obi could feel the animal's hot, angry breath on his face. He curled his fingers round the leather pouch hanging from his neck and could feel the hard shiny fact hidden inside. The pouch felt warm and comforting. Obi held his breath and waited for the lion to pounce.

But Boss didn't pounce. Instead he took a step

back. Then he took a deep breath and let it out slowly.

'Thank you boys,' he said. 'I almost lost it there.'

'Boss sometimes lets his emotions get the better of him,' explained Tickles. 'He's got anger management issues.' The Big Cats nodded their heads in agreement.

Boss stared at Obi. 'You are a very lucky monkey,' he said in a low, chilling voice.

'You mean a very stupid monkey,' whispered Chaz under his breath.

Boss sniffed the air and looked round at the meadow. 'It seems that we have a disagreement here, wouldn't you say, boys?'

'Yes, Boss,' agreed the Big Cats.

Boss turned to face the lions, leopards and cheetahs. 'Would you agree that the Big Cats have made a perfectly reasonable request, gentlemen?'

'Very reasonable, Boss,' said the Big Cats.

'Yet this rude monkey says that the Big Cats are not being fair,' said Boss, jabbing his paw in Obi's direction. 'He says we should share the meadow with them.'

Tickles pushed his way to the front of the Big Cats. 'Let's eat them now, Boss,' he growled. 'Chimpanzee is my favourite lunch and there's a juicy one hiding over there behind the hippo.'

'Patience, Tickles,' said Boss. 'You're always thinking about your next meal. Just the other day you ate a whole giraffe for breakfast.'

'And I still had room for a couple of baboons,' said Tickles, licking his lips.

'I'm starving too, Boss, and I'm in the mood for some monkey lunch,' declared one of the leopards, staring menacingly at Misha.

Obi moved next to Misha and felt her small hand take his. 'Monkey tastes good,' hissed the leopard, with a glint in his eye. 'Though, sometimes you get their little bones stuck between your teeth.'

'All in good time, Anton,' said Boss. 'It seems we need to agree whose going to live on the meadow. We wouldn't want the animals to think that the Big Cats are unfair, would we?'

'No, Boss,' cried the Big Cats.

A smile spread across Boss's face as he noticed the football goals. 'Ah,' he beamed. 'I see that you animals play football. Excellent.'

The other animals looked at each other with puzzled expressions. What was Boss taking about?

'I'm afraid we don't understand,' said Engelbert, politely.

Boss stared at Engelbert. 'Well, I've come across some pretty old elephants in my time but I don't think I've ever seen one as old as you.'

'He must be five hundred seasons old,' said Tickles, and all the Big Cats roared with laughter.

'What's football?' asked Engelbert.

'You may be old, but you're obviously not stupid,' said Boss, winking at the Big Cats. 'Pretending you don't know what football is when you've got a football pitch with proper goals and nets right here on the meadow. Try pulling the other leg Dumbo.'

'But these have always been here,' cried Obi. 'We don't know what they're for. Engelbert said that mankinders put them here.'

'Mankinders! A likely story,' scoffed Boss. 'It's obvious that you play football on this meadow and that's very fortunate as the Big Cats love to play football. Isn't that so, gentlemen?'

'Yes, Boss,' cried the Big Cats.

'And we're very good at football,' said the lion. 'The Big Cats have never lost a game, have we boys?'

'Never, Boss.'

'No team has ever come close to beating us, have they lads?'

'No way, Boss.'

Boss turned to Rio. 'Tell the animals what the score was the last time we played a football match.'

'Twenty-six, nil to the Big Cats,' he said, with a toothy grin.

'Twenty-six, nil,' purred Boss. 'We were playing the Meerkats from the savannah if I remember correctly. Zeff scored four goals, didn't you Zeff?'

'Five goals actually, Boss,' said the cheetah, proudly.

'Anton ate the Meercats goalkeeper,' Rio pointed out.

'Ah yes,' said Boss, 'perhaps eating our opponents' goalkeeper was not strictly within the rules, but it was an excellent team performance. The score speaks for itself . . . Big Cats twenty-six ... Meerkats nil.'

The animals of the meadow stood quietly, wondering what the Big Cats were talking about?

'And I'll give you one guess who the manager of the Big Cats team is,' said Boss. 'That's right, it's me,' he declared, without waiting for a reply. 'I choose the team . . . I decide the tactics . . . I'm the one in charge. Right boys?'

'Yes Boss,' roared the Big Cats, in one voice.

Boss stared at the animals of the meadow who stood huddled together. 'Which one of you is the manager?' he demanded.

The animals looked at each other blankly. 'I don't think we have a manager,' said Engelbert, eventually.

'You must have a manager!' cried Boss. 'Every football team has a manager.'

'But, we don't have a football team,' Gina the giraffe pointed out, politely.

'We don't know anything about football,' added Zoe the zebra.

Well, then,' said Boss, with a smile on his face, 'you'd better learn quickly, because in three moons the Big Cats will return to play a football match against

81

the animals of the meadow.'

The animals looked at one another anxiously.

'So, here's the deal. I give you my word that if you win the match, the Big Cats will leave the meadow and you'll will never see or hear from us again.'

'But what happens if you win?' said Obi.

'If the Big Cats win,' said Boss grinning, 'then you and your friends must leave the meadow and never return. Anyone who stays will be served up for the Big Cats lunch.'

'Or breakfast,' growled Tickles, licking his lips.

'Or dinner,' roared Rio.

'In three moons from now the referee's whistle will blow,' cried Boss, 'and a game of football will begin. The Big Cats versus the animals of the meadow.'

Boss raised his face to the sky. 'Winner takes all!' he roared.

Then, just as quickly as they had arrived, the Big Cats were gone. Following Boss, they raced off into the tall grasses at the end of the meadow in a whirlwind of teeth, claws, whiskers and fur.

Chapter 12
THE RULES

'We're done for!' shrieked Chaz, jumping up and down, slapping the top of his head with his hands. 'We've got to leave the meadow straight away. If we stay here we'll be eaten by the Big Cats.

'How can we win if we don't know anything about football?' said Jengo the gorilla, shaking his head. 'We don't stand a chance.'

'We have to get out of here' yelled Chaz. 'Did you hear what that lion said? Chimpanzee is his favourite lunch!'

'Where would we go?' asked Zoe. 'Obi is right . . . the meadow is our home. I've lived here my whole life.'

'But Chaz is right too,' said Herman the hippo, in a solemn voice. 'If the Big Cats have never lost a football match, they're bound to beat us and then we'll have to leave the meadow.'

'They won their last match 26-0!' cried Barney.

'And they ate the Meerkats goalkeeper,' added Becky.

'What's a goalkeeper?' asked Gina.

'Three moons,' groaned Engelbert. 'Boss said they'd be back in three moons.'

'Winner takes all,' grunted Walter. 'Isn't that what he said?'

'What if we talk to them nicely?' suggested Zoe,

hopefully. 'If the Big Cats see that we're nice and friendly, perhaps then they'll leave us in peace. Obi was right, there's room on the meadow for everyone.'

'I don't think talking to them nicely would do any good,' said Engelbert. 'Those Big Cats look as if they'd rather eat us than listen to our point of view.'

'Did you see the lion with the huge scar on his face?' said Gina, with a shudder. 'I don't ever want to meet him again.'

'Enough of this crazy talk,' yelled Chaz. 'You're all mad if you think we can stay here. The Big Cats have given us a chance to leave and I'm not hanging around here waiting to be gobbled up by a lion. No way . . . I'm out of here.'

The animals fell silent. They gazed solemnly at the soft grass, at the trees and the lake, at the purple hill and the beautiful flowers scattered across the meadow. This had been their home for as long as they could remember, but they knew in their hearts that Chaz was right. They would have to leave the meadow before the Big Cats returned - all those lions, leopards and cheetahs, with sharp claws and even sharper teeth.

Engelbert shook his head. 'We don't have any choice. Tomorrow, when the sun rises, we must leave and find another meadow,' he said, putting on a brave face.

The animals all nodded in agreement.

'Things might be different if we knew about

football,' said Herman. 'Maybe then we'd be able to stay.'

Just then there was a frantic flapping of wings and Paulie screeched and squawked above their heads, before coming to rest on the crossbar.

'I know all about football! As I told Obi, I once lived in a mankinder's house in a faraway place called London. I was locked in a cage and had to watch television all day.'

'Engelbert has told us about mankinders,' said Gina, 'but what does this have to do with football?'

Paulie jumped along the crossbar. 'That's what I'm trying to tell you! The mankinder watched football all day long. Football, football, football! It nearly drove me bananas I can tell you. I saw more football matches on that television than I care to remember. Match of the Day .... Champion's League ... Sky Sports. Hardly a day passed without the mankinder shouting at the television ... *Come on City!* .... *Get your eyes tested referee!* .... *He's a mile offside!* ... *Gooooaaal!*'

'Wait a minute,' said Misha, interrupting Paulie. 'Are you telling us that you know about football?'

'Know about football? Know about football?' squawked the parrot. 'I've seen more football matches than any parrot in the history of the world. I must have watched a thousand matches while I was trapped inside that beastly cage. Oh yes, I know all about football . . . listen . . I can prove it to you . . .'

Paulie paused for a moment to clear his throat. *'City's defence are at sixes and sevens this afternoon.... But wait a minute ... the striker's one-on-one with the keeper! ... Is this a last gasp equalizer? ... He's about to pull the trigger ... he's going for the top corner ... oooh he's missed a sitter ... an absolute sitter . . . United are over the moon .... City are sick as parrots .... Now back to Gary in the studio.'*

The animals stared at Paulie in astonishment. Then Gina stepped forward. 'Can you teach us about football?' said the giraffe, peering down at Paulie. 'Can you show us what to do?'

'Can you explain the rules?' said Herman.

'How do you win at football?' asked Jengo.

'What's a goalkeeper?' cried Walter.

'Don't all shout at once,' squawked Paulie. 'We're not going to get very far if you all ask me questions at the same time.' He hopped along the crossbar, his head bobbing up and down. 'If you listen quietly, I'll do my best to explain how to win a football match.'

'We'll be quiet,' promised Zoe.

The animals listened as Paulie started to tell them everything he knew about football. 'There are two teams in a football match and each team has eleven players . . .'

'How many is eleven?' asked Obi. 'I can only count to three.'

'Count all your toes and add one,' yelled Chaz,

slapping the top of Obi's head. 'I don't know why I'm even listening to Paulie. . . we have to get out of here *now.*'

'Oh, be quiet, Chaz,' said Misha. 'Let's hear what Paulie has to say.'

Paulie continued. 'Each player in a football team has a different job to do. The striker's job is to score goals . . . the defender's job is to stop the other team from scoring goals.'

'What do you mean, score a goal?' asked Gina.

'It means the attacking team has managed to get the ball between the defending team's goal posts,' squawked Paulie, kicking one of his scaly legs as if he was scoring a goal. 'It means they've put the ball past the goalkeeper, over the goal line and into the back of the net. That's what a goal is.'

'What are goal posts?' asked Barney.

'You're looking at them,' said Paulie, nodding at the wooden uprights and crossbar that he was perched on. 'These are the goalposts, and these string nets catch the ball when a goal is scored.'

'What's a ball?' asked Becky.

'Ah, yes,' said Paulie. 'I forgot to mention the ball. That's the whole point of the game. The ball is what the players kick with their feet. That's why the game is called *foot . . . ball.*'

'What does a ball look like?' asked Zoe.

Paulie closed his eyes and thought for a moment.

'It's quite hard to describe if you've never seen one. A football is round and looks a bit like a coconut.'

'Did you say a coconut?' asked Engelbert.

'Yes, just like a coconut,' said Paulie, 'except a football bounces when you kick it but coconuts don't bounce at all.'

'Wait a minute,' cried Engelbert. 'This is all starting to make sense.'

The animals stared at the elephant. 'What do you mean, Engelbert?' said Misha.

'That was what the mankinders were doing all those years ago,' explained Engelbert. 'Remember I told you about the day they ruined my birthday party? That's what the mankinders were doing. They were playing football.'

'As I was about to explain,' continued Paulie, 'the team that scores the most goals wins the match.'

'The Big Cats scored twenty-six against the Meerkats,' said Barney.

'Twenty-six, nil,' added Becky. 'The Meerkats didn't even manage to score one goal.'

'I can't remember any football team scoring twenty-six goals,' said Paulie. 'The Meerkats must have had a terrible defence.'

'They ate the Meerkats goalkeeper,' Walter reminded them.

'It's hard to stop the other team scoring if you haven't got a goalkeeper,' agreed Paulie.

Gina looked confused. 'Are you allowed to eat the other team's players?'

'Well, I can't say I ever saw that,' said Paulie. 'I imagine if you ate one of your opponents, you'd be sent off by the referee. A red card offence,' he added with a squawk.

'What's a referee?' asked Herman. 'Is he one of the players?'

'No, the referee isn't one of the players,' said Paulie. 'He's the judge of a football match. The referee makes sure that both teams play fairly and obey the rules. He blows a whistle if one of the players does something wrong. Then it's a free kick to the other team.'

'Twenty-six, nil' sighed Jengo. 'The Big Cats must be amazing at football.'

'They've never lost a match,' cried Chaz. 'That's a fact.'

'We wouldn't stand a chance against the Big Cats,' muttered Gina. 'We might as well pack up and leave now while we've still got the chance.'

The animals fell into a gloomy silence again, each of them trying to imagine life away from the meadow. Where would they go?

Obi stepped forward. 'We can't just give up without trying,' he said. 'If Paulie shows us what to do, and we practice every day, I'm sure we could learn to play football. Maybe we could beat the Big Cats after all.'

'Well, that's just the kind of dumb idea you'd expect

from a monkey,' yelled Chaz. 'You've never even learned to count past three, Obi, so how do you expect to learn to play football? Let's get out of here now and forget this stupid idea. I'm telling you for the last time, we can't play football against the Big Cats.'

'But we can learn,' insisted Obi. 'I'm sure if we practice ...'

'How can we practice?' said Becky. 'We don't have a football.'

'I'm not so sure about that,' said Engelbert, staring into the distance at the mpingo tree on top of the hill. 'I think I know where we might find one.'

Chapter 13
THE FOOTBALL

The animals had gathered under the mighty mpingo tree at the top of the hill. 'I wonder if it's still here,' said Engelbert peering up into the branches.

'I can't see anything,' said Olive the ostrich, craning and twisting her long neck to get a better look.

'This has to be the tallest tree I've ever seen,' declared Walter.

'Maybe your imagination is playing tricks on you, Engelbert,' suggested Zoe the zebra. 'The mankinders were here a very long time ago.'

Chaz pushed his way to the front impatiently. 'What a complete waste of time,' he cried. 'I don't believe you kicked the mankinders' football into this tree. I bet it's another of your made-up stories.'

'Are you sure it's there, Engelbert?' Misha asked.

'Yes,' replied the elephant. 'I'm certain it's still stuck in the highest branches.'

'Well, I can't see anything,' snapped Chaz.

'Maybe the wind blew it down?' suggested Herman.

'Perhaps it was a coconut after all,' said Becky.

'Well, there's only one way to find out,' said Gina. 'One of us has to climb the tree and try to find the football.'

The animals all turned to Chaz. 'What are you looking at me for?' he asked.

'Chimpanzees are the best climbers,' said Engelbert. The other animals nodded in agreement. 'Chaz, you must climb to the top of the tree and see if the football is still up there?'

Chaz slapped his head and jumped up and down. 'Climb the tree?' he yelled. 'You must be joking. A tree this high is far too dangerous to climb, even for me. One wrong step and it would be good-bye Chaz! There's no way I'm going to risk climbing the tree to look for some imaginary football.'

Engelbert turned to Jengo. 'What about you, Jengo? Can you climb this tree?' Jengo shook his head. 'Not me I'm afraid. I want to help but those high branches are far too thin for a gorilla to climb.'

Engelbert turned to the twin baboons. 'What about you guys?' he said. 'Baboons are very good climbers.'

'I'd like to ...' said Barney. 'Honestly I would, but I've got a bit of a problem with heights. I get dizzy even a little way off the ground.'

'Me too,' cried Becky.

'If no-one is willing to climb the tree, we'll never know if the football is still up there,' said Engelbert.

The animals stood in silence peering up into the branches of the tree, which was swaying gently in the afternoon breeze.

Obi stepped forward. 'I'll do it!' he cried. 'I'll climb the tree.'

The animals stared at him. 'You must be mad,'

shouted Chaz. 'One slip and you'll break your neck.'

'I know it's the highest tree on the meadow,' said Obi, 'but we must have a football to practice playing or we won't stand any chance against the Big Cats. Someone has to climb the tree so it might as well be me.'

The animals looked on as the little monkey began to climb. Before he got very far, Obi realised that someone was climbing the tree with him. He turned round to see Misha on the branch below.

'What are you doing?' said Obi.

'If you're going to climb the tree, I'm coming with you,' she said.

'But it's very dangerous.'

'I know,' said Misha, with an anxious smile, 'but together we can do it.'

Slowly, but steadily, the two monkeys climbed the mighty mpingo, clinging onto the branches with their hands and feet. The higher they went, the thinner the branches became and it was much more difficult to climb. But on they went until the meadow was far below them.

'We're getting near the top,' said Obi at last.

'Can you see the football? Misha asked.

Obi climbed higher and felt as if he was at the top of the world. He noticed how tiny his friends on the meadow looked. Even the lake seemed small. A hawk circled the tree, coming so close that Obi could almost reach out and touch it. In the distance he could see clouds of white steam rising above the canopy of the jungle.

'There doesn't seem to be anything in the branches,' shouted Obi. 'Nothing that looks like a football anyway.'

'Be careful,' called Misha. 'Those branches are very thin.'

Suddenly there was a loud crack as the branch Obi was standing on snapped. He lost his balance and fell backwards, tumbling down, desperately trying to grab hold of a branch as he did so. Misha screamed and tried to reach Obi's hand as he fell past her, but in the blink of an eye the little monkey had plunged into the green foliage below.

As Obi plummeted towards the ground, something amazing happened. Suddenly he stopped, suspended in mid air as if by magic, his arms and legs spread out like the sails of a windmill. He grabbed the nearest branch and pulled himself to safety, breathing a huge sigh of relief. He reached for the pouch to check that it was still hanging round his neck with the Fact safely inside. The pouch felt hot in his hand and it seemed to be glowing.

Misha could scarcely believe her eyes. 'Obi!' she yelled. 'You're okay!'

Obi smiled. 'Yes, I am.'

Misha gave Obi a huge hug. 'What happened? I

thought you were going to fall all the way to the ground.'

'I don't really know,' said Obi, looking perplexed. 'Everything happened so fast.'

'Well, you're one very lucky monkey,' said Misha, softly. 'And I think you're the bravest animal on the meadow.'

But Obi wasn't listening to Misha. Something had caught his eye, something old and tattered, and shaped like a coconut. There, wedged between two branches of the mpingo tree, was Engelbert's football.

Chapter 14

UNITED

Engelbert looked pleased. 'I knew it was still up there,' he said.

The animals inspected the old football that Obi had brought down from the tree.

'It's not the least bit like a coconut,' muttered Chaz.

'Well, it looked like a coconut to me,' said Engelbert. 'How was I to know it was a football?'

Paulie hopped onto the football and gave it some sharp pecks with his beak. 'It doesn't look like any football I've ever seen,' he croaked. 'The ones I saw on TV were white and shiny. This one's brown and wrinkly . . . a bit like Engelbert.'

The animals laughed, but Engelbert wasn't amused. 'We shouldn't be standing around making jokes,' he said sternly. 'We haven't much time before the Big Cats return. Now we have a football, we need to learn how to play.'

Herman pushed his way to the front. 'If you know about football Paulie, you must tell what to do. Can you show us how to play this game?'

'I've only watched football on TV,' croaked the parrot. 'I've never actually *played* football. What you need is a manager ... someone to teach you how to play as a team.'

Obi stepped forward. 'What about you, Paulie?' he

cried. 'Why can't you be our manager? No one else here knows anything about football. Please Paulie, it's our only chance of beating the Big Cats.'

'Well, I suppose I could,' said Paulie, surveying the eager group of animals in front of him. 'I can teach you the rules of football, but there are tactics to be considered as well.'

'What are tactics?' said Walter.

'Every team needs a game plan,' said Paulie.

'I don't understand?' said Zoe. 'What's a game plan?'

Paulie cocked his head to one side. 'Well, we have to plan how our team is going to play the match,' croaked the parrot. 'We must decide whether we're going to play with a flat back four or have our full backs pushing up and down the line.' Paulie cocked his head to the other side and gave the question some more thought. 'Or maybe we should go four-four-two with a holding midfielder . . . or play a lone striker up front. Oh, yes my friends, a game of football has a lot to do with tactics.'

The animals looked baffled. 'What's a full back?' said Jengo.

'What's a striker? asked Gina.

'What's four-four-two?' demanded Olive.

'I'm confused,' cried Zoe. 'You haven't even told us what we're supposed to *do* with this football.'

'Stop, stop ... don't all shout at once!' shrieked Paulie, flapping his wings furiously. 'We've a lot of hard work to do. In three moons the Big Cats will return and we must be ready for them. There are skills you need to learn, and learn quickly my friends. You need to know how to pass to each other, how to head the ball, how to tackle, how to shoot. We must learn how to attack and defend . . . how to spring the offside trap.'

'You're crazy,' yelled Chaz, waving his arms. 'There's no way we can learn all that in time. Even a team of chimpanzees, who are by far the cleverest animals on the meadow, wouldn't stand a chance against those Big Cats. How do you think a team of dumb monkeys, fat hippos and bungling baboons is going to win?'

'We have to try, Chaz,' Obi said quietly. 'I know I'm not intelligent, but I'm sure I could learn to play a game of football. With Paulie as our manager, we could all learn.'

'Obi's right,' cried Gina.

'We *can* learn to play football,' agreed Herman.

'I'll be the goalkeeper,' declared Jengo.

'I'll be a back full,' cried Barney.

'It's a full back, you idiot!' corrected Becky.

'We don't have a moment to spare,' said Engelbert. 'Come on Paulie, let's get started.'

'There's something we have to agree first,' said Paulie. 'We need to decide what we should call ourselves. Every football team must have a name, like . . . Rhinoceros Rovers ... or Warthog Wanderers ... Antelope Athletic .... or Real Rabbits.'

The animals stood quietly, each trying to think of a name for their team. Then Misha spoke. 'We may be different animals, but there's something that unites us all.'

'What's that?' said Engelbert.

'The *meadow*, of course! This is where we live. This is the home we all share.'

'We won't be sharing anything if those Big Cats move in,' said Chaz.

'Misha's right,' said Paulie. 'And we only stand a chance if we are *united*.'

Obi's face lit up. 'We should be called Meadow United.'

'Meadow United,' chorused the animals.

'That's an excellent name,' agreed Paulie. 'Meadow United, I like that.'

Obi felt proud. It was the first time he'd ever had a clever idea, and recently there were lots of other things he'd done for the first time. Standing up to Boss was the first time he'd shown courage, and climbing to the top of the mpingo tree was the first time he'd felt brave enough to go so high.

Obi knew that something had changed since his adventure in the jungle, but he wasn't sure what. He touched the pouch hanging from his neck and felt the fact inside.

'Meadow United?' said Chaz, in a mocking tone. 'That's a rubbish name. I can think of much better names than that.'

'Don't pay any attention to Chaz,' said Misha. 'I think Meadow United is a wonderful name. It shows that we are all in this together.'

'That's settled then,' said Engelbert. 'Meadow United will be the name of our football team.'

'Meadow United!' chorused the animals.

'Game on!' squawked Paulie. 'Meadow United versus the Big Cats!'

Chapter 15
THE MISSING MINERS

Emily Jackson wiped the sweat from her forehead and smiled for the television camera. The cameraman zoomed in on her face, while the sound engineer held the boom microphone and adjusted the sound levels.

'Okay guys, I'm good to go,' she said.

'And .... action!' cried the director.

Emily smiled and began talking to the camera. 'It was through jungle just like this that the explorers travelled all those years ago,' she said, gesturing with her hand at the tangle of roots and vines around her. 'On they walked, day after day, where no-one had ever set foot before, cutting a path through the jungle with their machetes.'

Emily paused for a moment and looked up at the huge trees that surrounded the film crew. 'Here, in the deepest part of the African jungle, trees grow so high that no light reaches the forest floor and it's difficult to tell if it's day or night.'

'Let's try sticking to the script, Emily,' said the director, interrupting her. 'It's not a wildlife documentary we're filming . . . it's a programme about the missing miners, remember?'

Emily pushed her long dark hair back from her face. The noise of the screeching birds and buzzing insects made it difficult to think clearly. She closed her eyes and tried to imagine what it would have been like for the miners, cutting their way through the dense jungle, hacking with machetes at the roots and vines to create a path. Leading the way was her grandfather, Edward Jackson, who had disappeared in the jungle many years before she was born. He had set off on the expedition in the summer of 1936 with twenty-two men and they had all disappeared in mysterious circumstances. Not one of them had returned.

More than seventy years later, she was following in her grandfather's footsteps, making a documentary called 'The Missing Miners.' Despite the heat of the jungle, Emily shivered. It was as if she could sense the ghosts of the lost explorers around her. What had happened to her grandfather and the other men? That's what they were there to find out.

Emily reached into the top pocket of her jacket and took out a piece of paper. In the pale sunlight that filtered through the trees, it was just possible to make out the lines of a map.

Emily held the map up to the camera and continued her report. 'This is the map that Edward Jackson and his men used. Before he left, Edward made a copy of it and hid it in the family vault where it lay undiscovered for many years. Legend has it that the map leads to a meadow, deep in the heart of Africa, where there are diamonds, far below the purple-coloured rocks and the red soil.

Emily stopped and looked at the jungle around her. For the briefest moment she thought she felt the ghostly hand of her grandfather on her shoulder. Shivering again, she continued. 'According to the legend, deep below the meadow lies the biggest diamond the world has ever seen. A stone larger than a man's fist . . . a magical diamond which shines with all the colours of the rainbow and sparkles like a thousand dancing stars.'

Emily put the map back in her pocket. She smiled once more for the camera. 'This is Emily Jackson for Channel 7 News, on day four of our journey in search of The Missing Miners of 1936.'

'And ..... cut!' cried the director.

Chapter 16
THE TRAINING SESSION

The training session was not going well. From his perch on top of the old wooden hamper Paulie flapped his wings furiously and screeched orders at the players.

'No, No, No! Not like that!' he squawked, at the top of his voice.

'Herman ... you're meant to kick the ball, not stand on it!'

'Zoe ... you're going the wrong way!'

'Walter ... stop eating the grass, you're supposed to be playing football!'

But it was no use. The animals of the meadow couldn't pass, they couldn't tackle, they couldn't head the ball and they couldn't shoot. They couldn't score a single goal.

Every time Herman tried to kick the ball he fell on his huge bottom, making the whole meadow shake as if there had been an earthquake.

'That's against the rules,' yelled Paulie, as the twin baboons wrestled for the ball. Barney gathered it in his long hairy arms and bounced it off his sister's head. Becky grabbed the ball from him, but then ran straight into the goal posts and fell dizzily to the ground.

Jengo sat on the crossbar examining his toes. 'What are you doing?' cried Paulie, with an exasperated squawk. 'You're supposed to be the goalkeeper but you won't to stop anyone scoring if you sit *on top* of the goals.'

'What's the point?' Jengo shouted back. 'I've been standing in goal all morning and I haven't had even one shot to save. This lot couldn't score a goal if their lives depended on it.'

'Actually, our lives *do* depend on it,' panted Engelbert. The old elephant was finding it difficult to run more than five paces without getting completely out of breath.

'You have to show a bit more backbone Olive!' screamed Paulie, as Olive the ostrich buried her head in the red soil every time the ball came near her.

'Olive's terrified of the ball,' Misha explained.

'I don't blame her,' said Chaz. 'I've already been smacked in the face by that stupid ball and it was very painful.'

'Gina . . . where are you going?' screeched Paulie, as Gina wandered off to munch some leaves from a nearby eucalyptus tree. 'You're our centre back ... that means you've got to defend the goal. You can't just leave the pitch whenever you feel hungry!'

'I'll be back in a bit,' said Gina, chewing away contentedly.

'I'm totally confused,' said Zoe, with a glazed expression. 'There are too many rules in football . . . offside . . . corner kicks . . . throw ins . . . goal kicks . .

. free kicks. How can anyone remember all these rules?'

Paulie closed his eyes and gave a long exasperated squawk. It was never like this on *Match of the Day*. The animals of the meadow were hopeless at football, every single one of them, and the worst player of all was Obi. The little monkey got so excited that could hardly run two steps without tripping over his feet. Paulie could see that he was trying his hardest, but he slipped and stumbled and missed the ball completely whenever he tried to kick it. Obi just wasn't any good at football.

Play stopped and all the animals stared impatiently at Walter. Somehow the ball had become wedged between the tusks of Walter's long snout. He was shaking his head furiously, but the ball was well and truly stuck.

'What do the rules say about that?' demanded Zoe.

'How are we meant to play without a ball?' asked Herman.

'That's a clever trick,' said Gina. 'The Big Cats won't score many goals if Walter keeps the ball jammed between his tusks.' The animals laughed at Walter's desperate efforts to dislodge the ball.

'Oh dear,' sighed Paulie.

It was then that the animals of the meadow noticed they were being watched. Standing quietly in the shade of the mpingo tree were three animals. One was the unmistakable figure of Boss, his thick mane blowing in the gentle meadow breeze. Behind him stood a mangy, longhaired hyena with large pointed ears and a black muzzle. He had something hanging from a piece of string round his neck.

The third animal was a huge cat, which it stood motionless beside Boss. He had orangey red fur with black stripes, but his throat was as white as the clouds in the sky. He flicked a football casually from one paw to the other.

'I wonder what they want,' said Gina, in a hushed voice.

'Looks like we'll find out pretty soon,' said Engelbert, as the three animals emerged from the shadows and made their way across the meadow.

Chapter 17

FANCY TRICKS

'You've been practicing,' Boss observed. 'I'm pleased that you're taking our challenge seriously. The match is only two moons away.'

The animals of the meadow stared nervously at their visitors, especially the one with the football. They'd never seen such a huge beast.

'But practising won't make much difference,' continued Boss. 'As I told you before, the Big Cats have never lost a football match.'

'One hundred per cent record, Boss,' said the hyena. Saliva dribbled from his long dark tongue.

Boss looked at Walter who was still shaking his head furiously from side to side. 'What, might I ask, does that ridiculous warthog have on his snout?'

'That's our football,' Obi explained.

'It doesn't look like a football.' Boss stepped forward to inspect the ball more closely. 'It looks more like a wrinkled old melon,' scoffed the lion.

'It's very old,' Obi explained, 'and it's been stuck at the top of a tree for many seasons.'

Boss swatted some flies with his thick brown tail. 'I want you to meet Bex,' he said. 'He's our star player and I brought him along to demonstrate some of his football skills.'

Bex flicked the ball above his head. Standing on his

back legs, he skillfully headed the ball a dozen or more times, and then juggled it from one paw to the other, without dropping it once. He launched the ball high into the air, catching it on the back of his neck where it balanced for a few moments, before he let it drop to the ground where it landed right beside his front paw.

The animals stared in astonishment. How was it possible to do such things with a football? A group of young monkeys clapped and cheered.

'Well done, Bex. A fine display of footballing skills,' said Boss.

'Bex is a superstar,' said the hyena. 'He's the best footballer in the world.'

Bex sniffed the air with his long nose. There were patches of white fur above his fierce yellow eyes. He snarled at the animals and the sight of his razor sharp fangs made them all take a step back.

Although he was frightened, Obi stepped forward. 'Excuse me Boss,' he began.

'It's *you* again,' said Boss, glaring over his whiskers, 'the monkey that can't stop talking. You had a lucky escape the other day when I nearly lost my temper with you.'

'I was just wondering,' Obi continued politely, 'what kind of animal is Bex? Is he a lion?'

'A lion?' Boss opened his mouth and roared with laughter. 'Bex is a tiger. He comes from Asia, which is a long way away.'

'He's a Bengal tiger,' added the hyena.

'What is he doing here?' asked Engelbert. 'How did a Bengal tiger end up in the African jungle?'

'He escaped from a traveling circus,' said Boss. 'We found him at our water hole one afternoon and when he joined in a practice match we discovered that he was an amazing football player, so we invited him to join the Big Cats team.'

'He doesn't say much, does he?' observed Herman.

'Bex does his talking with his feet,' cackled the hyena. 'He's the best footballer in the world. You'll find out soon enough, though. Bex will score loads of goals against you.'

Boss turned to the tiger. 'Bex, why not give these animals a further demonstration? Perhaps you could take a shot at the goal.'

'Go on Bex,' barked the hyena. 'Show these animals what you can do.'

The tiger moved gracefully onto the football pitch, rolling the ball in front of him. He stopped at the centre circle and turned to face the goals. In the distance, Jengo was still sitting on the crossbar examining his toes.

'Why is there a gorilla sitting on the crossbar?' asked Boss.

'That's Jengo,' said Obi. 'He's our goalkeeper and he likes to sit up there.'

'He might stand a better chance of saving the ball if

he stands between the goalposts, rather than sitting on top of them.'

'I'll save it, don't you worry,' shouted Jengo defiantly, swinging down from the bar. 'I haven't let in a single goal all morning,' he declared proudly, beating his chest with his fists.

'That's because there haven't been any shots at goal,' squawked Paulie.

'I'll stop that tiger from scoring,' said Jengo, taking up his position in the middle of the goals and stretching out his long arms. 'He might have some fancy tricks, but football is about scoring goals,' he boomed. 'Bex won't score any goals against me!'

Boss grinned. 'Your goalkeeper is very sure of himself. I'm sure Bex will be delighted to accept his challenge.'

Bex stood silently in the centre of the pitch. His flashing yellow eyes were fixed on Jengo, who was jumping up and down, beating his chest. 'Come on, come on!' yelled Jengo. 'Give me your best shot!'

'No one can score from that far away,' whispered Barney.

'It must be fifty paces,' said Becky.

'More like sixty,' said Gina. 'That ball will never reach the goal.'

But the animals of the meadow were amazed when the tiger took a step forward and smashed the ball towards the goal. It flew like a speeding bullet, straight into Jengo's stomach, knocking the gorilla off his feet and sending him flying backwards into the net. He landed with a thump on his backside, tangled in the net and gasping for air.

The tiger thrust a paw into the air to celebrate his goal. The gang of young monkeys clapped and cheered in excitement.

'What are you cheering for, you idiots?' screeched Paulie. 'Don't you know that he will be playing *against* our team.'

'What a strike!' cried the hyena. 'No keeper in the world could have saved that.'

'Thank you, Mr Herbert,' said Boss as he put a large paw on the hyena's shoulder. 'How rude of me, I haven't introduced you all to Mr Herbert. He has kindly agreed to referee our match.'

'He's going to be the referee?' said Engelbert, looking at the hyena suspiciously.

'Yes,' replied Boss. 'Mr Herbert referees all our matches, don't you?'

'That's correct, Boss,' said the hyena. 'Er . . I mean Lionel.'

'Mr Herbert will ensure that the match is played fair and square, with no cheating and no unfair tackles.'

'Fair and square, Boss' said the hyena, nodding.

'Mr Herbert knows all the rules.'

The hyena placed the whistle between his thin lips and a piercing blast sent a flock of startled kingfishers shooting high into the air.

Pheeeeeeep!

'Rule 44, section 12, states that nets must be properly attached to the goals,' he barked, pointing towards Jengo. The gorilla was still trying to disentangle himself from the netting which had become detached from the goal posts.

Pheeeep! The hyena blew his whistle again. 'That net must be repaired before the start of the match or else I'll award a bonus goal to the Big Cats.'

'You can't do that,' protested Paulie. 'There's no such rule.'

Pheeeeep! The hyena blew an even louder blast on his whistle and produced a yellow card which he waved at Paulie. 'I'm booking you for dissent,' he barked.

'But the match hasn't even started yet,' squawked Paulie.

'That's your last warning,' said the hyena. 'Any more cheek and you're off. It'll be a red card next time.'

'But you can't send me off,' protested Paulie. 'I'm the manager, not one of the players.'

'You're the manager?' Boss roared with laughter. 'A parrot?'

'Er . . . yes,' croaked Paulie, putting on his bravest face.

'Paulie knows everything about football,' said Obi. 'He's teaching us the rules.'

'Well, let that be a warning,' said the hyena. 'If

anyone breaks the rules, they'll be sent off. I'm not going to stand for any bad behaviour.'

'I think they've got the message, Mr Herbert,' Boss interrupted. 'You are firm but fair.'

'Firm but fair, Boss,' echoed the hyena.

'Well, we mustn't interrupt your practice any longer,' said Boss, with a smile. 'The match is only two moons away and it's obvious you need all the practice you can get.'

Paulie puffed out his grey feathers and cleared his throat. 'Meadow United will be ready for the challenge,' he croaked, defiantly.

'Meadow United,' repeated Boss. 'An interesting name for a football team, don't you agree, Mr Herbert?'

'It doesn't matter what they call themselves,' cackled the hyena. 'The Big Cats will beat this lot by twenty goals at least.'

Misha moved close to Obi and whispered, 'I'm worried about Mr Herbert being the referee. I don't think he likes us very much.'

Taking one last look around the meadow, Boss addressed the animals. 'Yes my friends, the Big Cats are certainly going to enjoy living here.'

Pheeeeeeep! With a final blast from Mr Herbert's whistle, Boss, Bex and Mr Herbert disappeared into the trees.

Chapter 18
THE BEND IN THE RIVER

Emily and the film crew came to a bend in the river where the trees were so tall that the sun was no longer visible. The colour of the river had changed from green to inky black and the jungle was eerily silent. There was no birdsong, no insects buzzing and nothing moved.

Emily spotted the boots hidden among the tangled roots of a tree. Lying nearby them was a tattered old hat.

'Hey, look at these,' she said in an excited voice. 'I bet these boots belonged to one of our miners. Maybe this was Jackson's hat?'

'It's just some old boots, Emily,' sighed the director. He sat down wearily on a tree trunk and scratched his head. 'I don't think it proves anything.'

'It proves that we're not the first people to be here,' said Emily.

'If you ask me, this whole trip is a waste of time,' groaned the cameraman. 'Five days tramping through the jungle and all we've got to show for it is a pair of old boots and a half-eaten hat.'

'We should turn back and get the first flight home,' muttered the sound engineer. 'I knew it was a bad idea to come on this trip.'

'I'm certain we're heading in the right direction,' said

Emily. 'Come on guys . . . let's give it a few more days. According to the map, we're getting close to the meadow. We can't give up now.'

'We've come all this way to Africa but still haven't managed to film any animals' said the director. 'Where are all the lions? We haven't seen any elephants or a single giraffe.'

'Wildlife films are ten a penny,' said the cameraman. 'It won't bother me if we don't see any lions or elephants.'

The engineer wiped his head and put his baseball cap back on. 'It's so bloomin' hot here. Even if we find your meadow, Emily, what are we going to do? The miners are long gone.'

'But don't you want to find out what happened to them?' said Emily.

'My guess is they just got lost,' replied the engineer. 'It would be dead easy to lose your way in this jungle. It all looks the same.'

'I agree,' said the cameraman. 'Sometimes I feel that we've just been going round in circles.'

'This part of the jungle does seem different, though,' said the engineer, wiping steam from his glasses as he inspected the trees around the little glade. 'It's strange . . . you can hardly hear a sound.'

'And the river's a different colour too,' said the cameraman. 'This place is pretty spooky.'

The director got to his feet. 'Okay Emily, we'll give it

two more days, but if we haven't found your meadow by then, I'm afraid we'll have to turn back.'

'Let's get going then,' said Emily, and the film crew continued cutting a path through the vines and creepers with their machetes.

'Did anyone notice the strange looking tree back there?' said the cameraman.

'You mean the yellow one with purple spots?' said the engineer.

'Weird,' said the cameraman.

Chapter 19
THE STRIKER

Obi was sitting on his favourite rock watching the evening sun cast long shadows across the meadow. Chaz was gathering palm nuts while telling Obi why chimpanzees are much better at football than monkeys.

'Chimpanzees have more skill,' Chaz declared. 'That's why Paulie is going to make me Meadow United's striker. He knows I'm brilliant at scoring goals.' Chaz kicked a stone and raised both arms into the air celebrating an imaginary goal. 'Chaz the chimpanzee strikes the ball powerfully and the shot is in the back of the net before the keeper makes a move!'

'I know you're much better at football than me,' said Obi, scratching his head, 'but I didn't see you score any goals at training today.'

'*Nobody* scored any goals,' snapped Chaz. 'But I'm the only one who *nearly* scored a goal, and I most certainly would have scored if that ridiculous tiger hadn't turned up to show off.'

'Bex is amazing at football,' said Obi, recalling the tiger's demonstration that afternoon. 'Mr Herbert says Bex is the best footballer in the world. Jengo never stood a chance of stopping that shot.'

'The tiger was lucky,' snorted Chaz. 'A proper goalkeeper would have saved it.'

Chaz climbed onto the rock and ate some palm nuts. 'Listen Obi, only a chimpanzee has enough skill to be a striker. A monkey could never be a striker. There wouldn't even be a monkey in the team if I was the manager.'

'I know,' agreed Obi, despondently. He watched some soldier ants scurrying about on the ground below and wondered if ants were better at football that he was.

'Monkeys are just not designed to play football,' said Chaz, continuing his lecture. 'Do you know that everyone was laughing at you today, Obi? You could hardly kick the ball without falling over. Even Misha was better than you.'

Obi stared down at his feet. 'I know,' he said. 'I really am useless at football.'

A group of young monkeys appeared on the path below them. They had painted orange and black stripes across their bodies and dyed the tops of their heads white. They all looked like tigers and sang as they skipped along the path.

Bex, Bex .... super Bex
Bex, Bex .... super Bex
Bex, Bex .... super Bex
Super Bex the Tiger!

'Idiots!' said Chaz. 'I don't know why they're so impressed with that tiger. It's me they should be cheering, not Bex. I am the star player of Meadow United. When Boss sees how good I am, I bet he'll ask me to join the Big Cats team.'

Obi remembered that the Big Cats would soon be returning to the meadow to play their match and the hairs on his tail stood on end. 'Do you think we have any chance against the Big Cats?' he asked.

Chaz frowned. 'Well, with me as striker, we will definitely score some goals,' he boasted. 'But the rest of the team are hopeless. Engelbert can't jump, Walter can't head the ball and Gina's legs get all tangled up whenever she tries to tackle. As for those idiotic twin baboons . . . they spend more time running after each other than chasing the ball. We've got about as much chance of beating the Big Cats as a monkey has of becoming intelligent.'

Obi gazed at the glowing orange sun, which was disappearing behind the huge mpingo tree at the far side of the meadow. He knew Chaz was right. It didn't matter how much they practiced, anyone could see that the Big Cats would win the match easily.

Just then the young monkeys reappeared on the path singing another song.

One Bex the Tiger!
There's only one Bex the Tiger!

One Bex the Ti-ger!
There's only one Bex the Ti-ger!

'Fools!' yelled Chaz, shaking his fist angrily and flinging a handful of palm nuts at the monkeys.

Then he sat back and spoke to Obi. 'I've been meaning to ask,' he said. 'What's that you've been wearing round your neck?'

Obi put his hand on the pouch and felt the stone inside. Ever since he had returned from the jungle he had had wanted to tell Chaz about his adventure, but something had stopped him. Obi had noticed that he felt different and could do new things whenever he wore the pouch round his neck. Yesterday, as he was gathering bananas for Chaz's breakfast, he was amazed to discover that he could count past three. He collected thirty bananas, just as he had promised Chaz he would ... twenty-seven ... twenty-eight ... twenty-nine ... thirty! Suddenly, he was able to count.

Although he didn't understand why this was happening, Obi felt that it was something to do with the pouch round his neck.

'Well?' demanded Chaz, impatiently. 'Are you going to tell me what it is?'

'It's just something I found in the jungle and I like wearing it. It makes me feel different.'

'It makes you look ridiculous,' sneered Chaz. 'As I've told you many times, there's nothing the least bit special about monkeys. I have never met a monkey that knows even one single fact.'

'But I do know some facts,' said Obi.

'Really?' said Chaz, a smile spreading slowly across his face. 'Go on Obi, why don't you share some of these facts with me?'

Obi closed his eyes and tried to remember all the things he had learned in the jungle about snakes and crocodiles.

'Come on, come on,' said Chaz, impatiently. 'Just one fact from your peanut-sized monkey brain.'

Obi took a deep breath. 'A crocodile is best at climbing trees .... No, wait .... a snake can stay underwater for three hours .... Yes, I'm sure that's right .... No, hold on .... crocodiles change their skins every year ..... Or was that snakes?'

No matter how hard Obi tried to remember what Sigmund and Carl had told him, all the facts were jumbled up in his head.

Chaz shrieked with laughter. He jumped up and down on the rock and slapped his head. 'A crocodile that can climb a tree. What nonsense!'

The chimpanzee clambered down the rock and bounded along the path. 'Ha, ha, ha ... just wait until I tell the others.'

Obi sat for a long time watching the sun go down and the moon rise above the meadow. Chaz was right. A monkey could never be half as clever as a chimpanzee. He made up his mind that from now on he would stop trying to become more intelligent.

As Obi was deciding which tree to sleep in that night, he noticed that the football pitch was lit up by the pale moonlight. He could see the football lying near the centre circle and it seemed to be calling to him. He climbed down and made his way to the pitch.

The little monkey stood for a moment staring at the ball. The pouch round his neck began to glow and the football pitch was suddenly lit up by a thousand coloured lights. Above his head, stars danced like tiny diamonds.

Obi flicked it the ball into the air. He headed it over and over again, and then juggled it from one foot to the other. Then, with a swing of his right foot, Obi smashed the ball at the goal. It flew like a bullet, straight into the net.

Obi picked up the ball and went back to the centre circle and did the same thing again.

And again.

And again.

And again.

Chapter 20
TEAM TALK

Thwack!

The ball flew past Jengo's outstretched arm and hit the back of the net. Goal!

The animals couldn't believe their eyes. Obi had just scored his ninth goal at that afternoon's training session. The little monkey had won the ball near the halfway line and dribbled past six players, before thundering a shot past Jengo.

Everyone was astonished at the change in Obi. Yesterday, he had been the worst football player on the pitch, but today he was far better than any of them. He was so skillful that no one managed to tackle him. Every time Obi had the ball, he scored a goal.

From his perch on the old crate, Paulie watched as Obi trapped the ball under his right foot, before taking off and speeding past the other players. Running faster than the meadow wind, he dribbled past the twin baboons and skipped over the lunging tackles of Gina and Walter. In the blink of an eye, Obi had taken the ball past the entire team and now he only had Jengo to beat. As the goalkeeper rushed out, Obi lobbed the ball skillfully over his head and into the net.

'What a goal!' screeched Paulie, taking off into the air and circling the pitch three times while cheering at the top of his voice. 'That's ten goals Obi's scored, and each better than the one before.'

The animals stared at Obi. 'How did you become so good at football?' asked Walter, shaking his head in amazement.

'Yesterday you were terrible,' said Zoe, 'But today, you're incredible.'

Obi said nothing. He smiled awkwardly and touched the leather pouch round his neck.

'Time out guys,' squawked Paulie. 'Let's have a team talk.'

The players gathered in a circle round the old crate. The low afternoon sun cast long animal-shaped shadows across the pitch. Gina the giraffe's shadow was so long that it reached far beyond the grasses and onto the high rocks beside the old mine.

Paulie was excited. He puffed out the grey feathers on his chest and began. 'Players of Meadow United,' he squawked, 'Obi has given us all a lesson in how to score goals. If we are going to beat the Big Cats that is what you must all do tomorrow. It's goals that win football matches . . . goals are the difference between winning and losing.'

Chaz sighed loudly. 'I don't know what all the fuss is about. Obi's goals were all lucky.'

'Lucky?' spluttered Paulie. 'Did you say lucky? I've never seen a better demonstration of goal scoring, not even on *Match of the Day*.'

'Obi scored ten goals,' said Zoe. 'You didn't even

score one goal, Chaz. The only thing you did today was complain that we don't pass the ball to you.'

'Well, what do you expect,' snapped the chimpanzee. 'I've hardly had a kick of the ball because that greedy monkey kept it to himself.' Chaz jabbed an accusing finger at Obi. 'Everyone knows a chimpanzee will score more goals than a beetle-headed monkey.'

'Come on guys,' said Engelbert. 'We're supposed to be a team. Tomorrow we play the Big Cats in the biggest challenge of our lives. We won't have any chance of winning if we argue amongst ourselves.'

'We won't win anyway,' muttered Chaz.

'I'm not so sure,' squawked Paulie. 'We are definitely getting better. Our passing is improving and our defence is stronger too.'

'And we have a player who can score goals,' boomed Jengo, putting a huge hairy arm round Obi. The other animals all agreed.

'I have no idea how he's suddenly become so good at football,' said Paulie, 'but with Obi in our team, maybe ... just maybe, we have a chance of beating the Big Cats after all.'

'I'm in the team?' gasped Obi in amazement. He couldn't believe that he was going to play against the Big Cats. It was the most exciting thing that had ever happened to Obi and his little face beamed.

But Chaz's face wore a very different expression. His lips curled back in a toothy snarl, his nostrils flared and his eyes were cold narrow slits, as dark as coffee beans.

Chapter 21

THE PHOTOGRAPH

It was late afternoon and the film crew decided to take a break so Emily took off her backpack and sat down by the river. Closing her eyes, she thought back to a time when she was at primary school and she'd ask her teacher endless questions about animals.

'Excuse me Miss,' she would say in her small, excited voice. 'Of all the animals in the world which is the fastest?'

'I don't know, Emily,' her teacher would sigh. Miss Bradley never seemed very interested in animals, but that didn't stop Emily asking the questions.

'Miss, which animal can jump highest? Which animal is cleverest? Which animal is strongest?' Miss Bradley never knew the answers to Emily's questions.

Emily remembered a lesson about the solar system, when she asked a question that didn't have anything to do with planets. 'Miss Bradley,' she cried, waving her hand in the air, 'which is more scary . . . a lion or a tiger?'

Miss Bradley had stared at Emily over the top of her glasses. 'How should I know which is more scary,' she replied. 'Perhaps you should go to Africa and find out!'

Emily opened her eyes and smiled at the memory. Miss Bradley would be proud of her now. She'd made it to Africa after all and she'd never lost her fascination for animals.

Emily opened her backpack and took out a small photograph. She sat for a while staring at the faded black and white image of her grandfather. It was the only picture she had of Edward Jackson and it had been used in the newspaper report about the missing miners.

"*Twenty-three Men Go Missing in Africa,*" was the headline in the Duncastle Gazette in September 1936. "*A group of diamond miners, led by Duncastle explorer Edward Jackson, has disappeared in the African jungle. Nothing has been seen of the men for more than three months and there are fears for their safety.*'

Emily stared at the photograph. Her grandfather had piercing blue eyes, a wide moustache, and a determined look on his face.

'What happened to you Edward Jackson?' she wondered. 'Did you ever find the diamond you were searching for?'

Chapter 22
SECRET WEAPON

It was late in the afternoon and the animals had taken a break from training.

'Okay, everyone,' said Paulie, 'we need to talk about tomorrow's match and who's going to be playing for Meadow United.'

Paulie jumped up onto the old wooden crate. 'Let's start with the goalkeeper.' The parrot's grey head swiveled towards Jengo the gorilla. 'You will be in goal for us tomorrow, Jengo. We're depending on you to stop the Big Cats from scoring any goals.'

'Yes, Paulie,' barked the gorilla, beating his chest with his huge fists. 'You can depend on me!'

Then Paulie turned to the twin baboons. 'Barney and Becky, you will be our full backs. You must tackle like demons and push up and down the line to support our midfield players.'

The twin baboons stepped forward together. 'We will, Paulie,' they chorused.

'Engelbert and Gina,' cried Paulie. 'You are our centre backs. Your job is to stop the Big Cats from getting near our goal. Gina, with your height, you must win everything in the air. Engelbert, it's your job to clear the ball from the danger area. Remember how far you were able to kick the ball when you were a baby elephant?'

'We'll do our best, Paulie,' said Gina. 'But aren't we forgetting about that tiger? Bex is the best football player in the world. He can score goals from anywhere.'

'Don't worry about Bex,' said Paulie, 'if the Big Cats don't get the ball to him, he won't be able to score any goals.'

'But how will we stop Bex from getting the ball?' asked Olive.

Paulie's head swiveled round and he blinked furiously. 'That's the job of Walter and Herman. They will be our midfield destroyers.'

'Yes, Paulie,' boomed the warthog and the hippo, standing shoulder to shoulder.

'You must make every tackle count and win every challenge so that Bex doesn't get the ball. Do you think you can do that?'

'We can!' promised Walter and Herman. 'The Big Cats won't know what's hit them.'

Paulie hopped sideways along the crate. 'Now we come to the wingers,' he squawked. 'Zoe and Olive, it will be your job to get to the line and send over crosses for our strikers. You must get the ball into the Big Cats penalty area so that our strikers can do their job.'

'Yes, Paulie,' chimed the zebra and ostrich, in harmony.

Paulie shuffled back along the crate. 'Now, we're not going to win this match unless we score at least one goal,' he said, cocking his head to one side. 'And that brings me to the attack. We need a target up front and that's going to be you, Chaz.'

The chimpanzee's eyes narrowed. 'What do you mean, *target*?' muttered Chaz, suspiciously. 'You said I was going to be the striker.'

Paulie cocked his head the other way. 'When we're attacking, our players will try to get the ball to you. You will be the target . . . your job is to draw in the Big Cat defenders and that will create space for Obi.'

The parrot hopped to the other end of the crate, his head bobbing up and down furiously. There was a gleam in Paulie's eyes as he continued. 'If you can get the ball to Obi, he will score the goals and we will win the match. Our magical monkey will be our secret weapon!'

Obi was glowing with pride at the thought of being Meadow United's secret weapon. He felt sure that as long as he was wearing the magical Fact in the pouch round his neck, he could do anything – even score a goal against the Big Cats!

Paulie wasn't finished. 'There is one position I haven't mentioned yet. All football teams must have a substitute in case one of our players gets injured, or if we need fresh legs later in the game. So, Misha, you will be Meadow United's substitute.'

'Are you sure?' said Misha, looking doubtful. 'I don't think I'm any good at football.'

'It's true, monkeys are rubbish at football,' sneered Chaz. 'With another monkey in the team we stand even less chance of winning.'

'Don't be so rude!' cried Zoe. 'Misha is just as good at football as you …'

Engelbert stopped the argument. 'We shouldn't be saying bad things about any of our players,' croaked the elephant. 'We're supposed to be a team. We should be encouraging each other. Apart from Obi, none of us are much good at football, but we have to try to work together.'

'Engelbert's right,' agreed Paulie. 'If we don't believe in each other, we might as well not turn up for the match tomorrow. We'll have lost before we even kick the ball.'

'Ignore Chaz,' Obi whispered to Misha. 'I'm glad you're in the team. You can take my place any time.'

Misha smiled. 'There's no way I can take your place, Obi. You're the only chance we have of winning.'

'Time for more practice,' squawked Paulie. 'We need to work on set pieces. Free kicks and corner kicks often decide the outcome of a football match. Okay everybody, let's get out there and practice!'

As the players made their way back onto the football pitch, Obi turned to Misha. 'Do you really think we can win tomorrow?' he asked.

Misha was quiet for a moment. The two monkeys watched as Walter passed the ball to Herman, who in turn passed it to Gina, who flicked it skillfully to Olive. 'That's the way!' screeched Paulie, flying above the players. 'Keep it moving . . . keep it moving . . . yes, very good. . . now we're playing like a proper football team.'

'I've no idea,' said Misha. 'None of us are much good at football . . . we're certainly not nearly as good as the Big Cats, and we haven't even played a proper match before. I'm also worried about that referee.

'I'm sure Mr Herbert will be fair,' said Obi. 'After all, he knows all the rules of football.'

'All we can do is try our best and hope that you can score some goals.'

'Come on,' shouted Obi, running back onto the pitch. 'The sun will be going down soon, so we need get practising.'

Chapter 23
THE LEGEND

'What else do you know about your grandfather?' the director asked Emily. It was almost nightfall and the film crew were pitching their tents in a small clearing.

Emily swatted some insects that were buzzing around her ears. 'Edward Jackson was the leader of the expedition, but not much else is known about him,' she replied. 'I visited Duncastle, the town where he came from, but the people there didn't seem to know much about him.'

'Had your grandfather been to Africa before?'

'Yes, lots of times. I think his last trip in 1936 was the tenth time he'd come here. Sadly his wife was killed in a bombing raid during the Second World War and their two children were brought up by an aunt. Legend has it that there was a curse on the Jackson family.'

'A curse,' said the director. He gave a low whistle. 'Do you think that might have something to do with the disappearance of the miners?'

'I've no idea,' said Emily. 'Something bad must have happened to them in this jungle, that's for sure.'

'How can twenty-three men just disappear?' said the engineer. 'You'd think some of them would have made it back home.'

'Well, this map was probably all they had to guide them.' said Emily.

'What about the story of the diamond?' the director asked. 'Do you think that's true?'

'Tell us about the diamond, Emily' said the engineer.

Emily took drink from her water bottle. 'Legend has it that during his first trip to Africa, Jackson met an old man begging for food. The man only had one leg and he told my grandfather that he'd lost a leg when he was attacked by a lion.'

'A lion?' said the engineer, looking round nervously. 'You don't think there are any lions here, do you?'

The director shook his head. 'You won't find lions in the jungle. I'm sure lions prefer open savannahs and grasslands.'

'So, what about the old man?' said the cameraman.

'My grandfather gave him some food and they talked long into the night. The man told Jackson about a secret meadow, deep in the heart of the jungle, where the biggest diamond in the whole of Africa was to be found. Jackson asked the old man to draw a map and then, I guess, he spent the rest of his life searching for the meadow and that diamond.'

'I doubt it existed in the first place,' said the cameraman. 'There's no way I'd spend year after year in this jungle just because of a crazy old man's story.'

Emily shrugged. 'Well, my grandfather certainly believed that the legend was true and that's why he returned to Africa so many times.' She hammered in the last peg of her tent and tightened the ropes. 'But there was one other thing my grandfather loved to do as much as searching for diamonds.'

'What was that?' asked the cameraman.

Emily laughed. 'He loved to play football! Edward Jackson had a reputation for being a really good player.'

'Football?' said the engineer. 'Well, Jackson wouldn't have been able to play much football in the jungle, would he?'

'I bet there isn't a football pitch within five hundred miles of here,' said the cameraman. 'I can't wait to get back home, put my feet up and watch *Match of the Day*. Haven't seen a decent game of footie for ages.'

Chapter 24

MAGICAL POWERS

As the last embers of orange sunlight disappeared behind the mpingo tree, Misha joined Obi on his favourite rock. For a while, neither of them spoke and the two friends gazed upon the darkening meadow.

'It's beautiful,' said Misha, breaking the silence.

Obi sighed. 'It's the most wonderful place I know.'

'You seem sad Obi. What's wrong?' Misha asked.

Obi looked at the darkening sky. The stars were bright above the meadow. 'I was just thinking that this could be the last night any of us spend on the meadow. If we lose the match tomorrow, we'll all have to leave. You . . . me . . . everyone.'

Misha frowned. 'Don't talk like that. What about all the goals you scored today? You were amazing, Obi. If you can play like that against the Big Cats tomorrow, I'm sure we could win.'

Obi fell silent. He stared at the dark shadows on the ground below. Absent mindedly, he closed his fingers round the pouch.

Misha moved closer to Obi. 'Do you want to let me in on your secret?' she asked, softly.

Obi was confused. 'What secret?' he asked.

Misha smiled. 'Well, you can start by explaining how you've become so amazing at football. You used to fall over every time you tried to kick the ball, but now you've become our best player. There's something you're not telling me, Obi.'

Obi closed his eyes and listened to the chorus of crickets in the long grass. 'It's got nothing to do with me, Misha. It's because of this,' he said, touching the leather pouch.

'The pouch?' said Misha. 'How's that got anything to do with how you play football?'

'I'm useless at football Misha, but when I wear this round my neck something special happens ... I don't know how to explain it.'

'Something special?' Misha said.

'I know it sounds weird, but when I wear this round my nick it makes me feel that I can do anything.' Obi pulled the ties over his head and opened the pouch. The diamond blazed like the sun and was hot in his hand.

'It's amazing!' gasped Misha. The lights danced in her eyes, making them look like they were on fire. 'What is it Obi? Where did you find it?'

'Do you remember I went to the jungle?' Obi began, relieved that he was finally able to tell someone about his adventure.

'Of course I do. You said you were searching for a tree that Chaz had told you about.'

'Yes, the Fact Tree,' said Obi, 'and I picked this from one of its branches.' Obi held the precious stone out for Misha to see.

'I still find it hard to believe there's such a thing as a Fact Tree,' said Misha. 'I don't know why you believe everything that chimpanzee tells you.'

'But just look at it Misha!' cried Obi. 'It's the biggest Fact in the world. I feel special when I wear it round my neck . . . as if I have magical powers.'

'Magical powers?' said Misha, turning the diamond over in her small hands. 'I knew you were different when you came back from the jungle. What happened there, Obi? You've got to tell me.'

As night descended on the meadow, Obi explained how the Fact had given him the courage to stand up to Boss and how it had helped him climb the mpingo tree when everyone else was too scared. It was because of the Fact that he could count past three and was able to think up the best name for their team. But the most important thing of all, Obi explained, was that wearing the fact made him skillful at football.

'Everyone knows I can hardly kick the ball properly, never mind score a goal,' said Obi. 'But something happens when I have this round my neck. I feel clever and brave. I'm able to do things that I only ever dreamed of doing.' He stopped and gazed up at the huge yellow moon rising above the meadow.

Misha put the diamond back into the pouch and pulled the ties over Obi's head so that it was hanging securely round his neck. 'I don't really understand,' she sighed, 'but I am sure of one thing, Obi . . . it's only because of you that Meadow United have any chance of beating the Big Cats.'

The two monkeys stayed on the rock for a while longer, watching the moon rise high above them in the night sky. They had no idea that in the shadows below, someone had heard every word.

Chapter 25
PHANTOM OF THE MEADOW

It was the middle of the night. The meadow was quiet and still, the silence broken only by the occasional call of a giant eagle owl and Engelbert's snoring. The yellow moon hung like a lantern in the night sky. Glow-worms glittered and hammer-nosed bats chased insects round the trunks of acacia trees.

But not everyone was asleep. A dark figure emerged from the long grasses and crept silently across the meadow, where it stopped at the bottom of a baobab tree. Slowly and quietly it climbed the tree until it reached Obi, who lay fast asleep. For a moment the figure froze as an eagle owl set off on its flight above the lake.

The figure continued, creeping along the branch until it reached the sleeping monkey. Nimble fingers reached out carefully for the strings of Obi's pouch and lifted it over his head. The little monkey's eyes fluttered briefly and his tail tightened round the branch, but Obi continued to sleep. The shadow retreated back along the branch and slipped down the tree. Speeding across meadow under cover of night, the phantom of the meadow disappeared back into the tall grasses.

Dark clouds rolled across the moon and a cool breeze fanned the sleeping animals. The first rush of wind over, raindrops as big as a palm nuts fell on the sleeping meadow. As the heavens opened and torrents of rain descended, it quickly covered the meadow in deep pools of water.

Suddenly there was a flash of light above the jungle canopy and an ear-splitting crack of thunder, which woke all the animals. A huge bolt of lightening struck Engelbert's mpingo tree, splitting it down the middle as if a giant axe had sliced it in two. As the tree crashed to the ground and exploded into flames, terrified animals ran for safety. It burned so fiercely that even the heavy rain didn't put out the flames.

In the darkness, amid the deafening roar of the thunderstorm, a small voice could be heard from a nearby baobab tree.

'It's gone!' wailed Obi. 'The Fact has gone!'

Chapter 26

THE BONES

'I think these bones are human,' said the cameraman, giving them a poke with his machete. 'But if there was a skull here, we'd know for sure.'

'Poor bloke, I wonder what happened to him,' said the engineer, taking off his baseball cap and scratching his head. 'Do you think he was one of the miners, Emily?'

The film crew had discovered the bones in a marshy area near some fig trees. Jackson's map had indicated they should follow the river, but last night's thunderstorm had made the banks slippery and dangerous to walk along. One false step would send them tumbling into the river so they had decided to abandon the river path and go through the jungle instead. Just before midday they made their discovery.

Emily inspected the pile of bones. 'I'm no expert,' she said, taking off her backpack. 'But if these are human bones, they almost certainly belong to one of the miners.'

The director crouched down to take a closer look. 'We're not going to get much information from this poor chap. I wonder what happened to him.'

'I wonder if it's Edward Jackson,' said the cameraman.

Emily shook her head. 'I can't explain why, but I

don't believe this is my grandfather.'

'What makes you say that?' asked the director, brushing a large spider from his trousers.

'I don't know,' said Emily. 'Just a feeling.'

Chapter 27

NOWHERE TO BE SEEN

The storm had passed and the sun was shining brightly on the meadow. The jungle was steaming like a witch's cauldron as the mist evaporated into a clear blue morning. The pools of rainwater had almost disappeared and the meadow smelled sweet and fragrant.

Many of the animals had gathered to inspect the charred and smoking remains of Engelbert's tree, while on the other side of the meadow, a very unhappy monkey was searching for a missing pouch.

'I've looked everywhere,' groaned Obi, in despair. 'It's just nowhere to be seen.'

'When did you last see the pouch?' Misha asked.

'I was wearing it when I went to sleep last night,' cried Obi, 'but when I woke up during the storm it was gone.' He shook his head miserably and his eyes started to fill with tears. 'I don't know what to do, Misha. Without the Fact, I'm useless.'

'Maybe the pouch fell from your neck while you were sleeping,' suggested Misha. 'Have you checked under the tree?'

'That's the first place I looked,' wailed Obi. 'I've searched everywhere, but I just can't find it.'

'It can't have just vanished,' said Misha, frowning. 'It must be somewhere and I'm sure we'll find it.'

'But the match is today!' cried Obi. 'The Big Cats will be here soon. What am I going to do, Misha? Without the Fact I'm no good at football ... the team will be better off without me.'

Misha put her arm round Obi. 'Everything will be okay,' she said. 'Listen Obi, it wasn't the Fact that scored all those goals yesterday . . . it was *you;* your feet dribbling the ball past the defenders, and your shots flying into the net. It was *you* scoring the goals, wasn't it Obi?'

'But you don't understand,' said Obi, waving his arms frantically. 'The Fact is magical . . . all I know is that when I'm not wearing it, I'm only a dumb monkey, just like Chaz says. I tried to count this morning, but I couldn't remember which number comes after three. I'm useless at everything.'

'You're not useless, Obi.'

'Yes I am! You were right when you warned me not to go to the jungle. If I hadn't found the Fact Tree, I wouldn't be so miserable now.'

'I'm glad you went to the jungle,' said Misha. 'You've done some amazing things since you got back.'

'That's what's so unfair,' cried Obi. 'For the first time in my whole life I believed in myself. I thought I could be clever and brave, just like my best friend Chaz. Now I'm just a dumb monkey again.'

Misha placed a hand gently on Obi's arm. 'You may not believe in yourself Obi, but I do. When you get out there on the pitch, I know you won't let Meadow United down. You are our striker . . . our secret weapon . . . and you're going to score lots of goals against those Big Cats.'

'Do you really think I can do that?' said Obi, his voice trembling.

'Yes, I do,' said Misha. 'And I can't wait to see Boss's face when you dribble past those Big Cats. There will be no stopping you.'

A loud squawk interrupted them. 'Team talk!' said Paulie, circling above their heads. 'The Big Cats will be here soon.'

Misha looked at Obi's sad face. 'You've got to forget about the Fact and concentrate on Meadow United,' she said softly. 'Everything will be fine. You'll see.'

Chapter 28
TEAM SPIRIT

The Meadow United players gathered to hear Paulie's final team talk. Nearby, a group of excited young monkeys were clapping their hands and singing loudly.

Who put the ball in United's net?
Bex did, Bex did
Who put the ball in United's net?
Bex the Tiger did.

Chaz shook his fist angrily. 'You lot won't be singing when I get my hands on you!'

The players stood in a circle round Paulie who was perched on top of the old crate. 'My friends, we are about to face the biggest challenge of our lives. We are playing a football match against the Big Cats which will decide the future of your lives here on the meadow.'

The animals listened in silence. It was only three days ago that the Big Cats had arrived on the meadow and issued their challenge, and in that time the animals had learned to play football. They could all pass the ball, tackle and shoot. They could attack and defend, and they understood the different positions and the job of each player in the team. They had stayed up late each night while Paulie explained the rules of football.

But their faces showed that they were all dreading the arrival of the Big Cats. They knew in their hearts that the Big Cats would be fearsome opponents - bigger, faster, stronger and more skillful than the players of Meadow United.

'Listen to me, everyone,' squawked the Paulie, his head swiveling round and his beady eyes blinking rapidly. 'We all know that the Big Cats are good at football.'

'They've never lost a match,' Herman pointed out, gloomily.

'They beat the Meerkats twenty-six, nil,' said Olive.

'And they have Bex, the best footballer in the world,' added Walter, with a grunt.

'We haven't got a hope of beating those Big Cats,' yelled Chaz. 'I vote we all get out of here while we still can.'

'Maybe this team talk wasn't such a good idea,' croaked Engelbert. 'It's not doing much for our confidence.'

Paulie gave an exasperated squawk. The team talk wasn't going as planned. He looked at Obi who didn't seem to be listening. He was slouching and staring glumly at his feet. Obi had hardly said two words since the storm. It wasn't like him to be so quiet.

Paulie cleared his throat and continued. 'I think we all agree that the Big Cats team is strong, but our team has strengths too.'

'We do?' grunted Walter. 'What are *our* strengths?'

Paulie's head bobbed up and down as he worked his way sideways along the edge of the crate. 'Team spirit!' screeched the parrot, his eyes blinking like scissors. 'That is Meadow United's greatest strength.'

The animals looked at each other blankly. 'What do you mean, Paulie?' asked Engelbert.

There was a gleam in Paulie's eyes. 'If the players in a football team believe in each other and are determined to win the match, then that team has *spirit*. Team spirit is just as important as being skillful or fast or strong. Sometimes a team can beat opponents who are better players because they have more spirit. It's like having an extra player in your team.'

'Team spirit,' said Gina, looking down on Paulie from her great height. 'That's our strength?'

'Yes it is!' screeched Paulie. 'We have much more team spirit than those Big Cats. We'll be fighting for our home and our future. All the animals on the meadow are depending on us and we can't let them down.'

'Paulie's right,' said Engelbert.

'There's one last thing I want to say,' squawked Paulie. 'Inside this old crate I think we'll find something that will give us even more team spirit.' Paulie pecked at the lid with his beak.

'That crate is older than Engelbert,' muttered Chaz.

'How can you possibly know what's inside?'

'Just a hunch,' said Paulie. 'Let's open it.' Paulie turned to Jengo. 'You're the strongest among us, can you open the crate?'

The animals watched as Jengo wrestled with the lid. Then, as the rusty hinges gave way, there was a splintering crunch and the lid tore open.

'Is there anything inside?' asked Misha.

Jengo reached inside with his long arms and pulled out the contents of the crate. The animals watched in amazement as the air was filled with dancing, multi-coloured shapes which fell to the grass in a jumble of reds, whites and blues.

'Skins!' gasped Engelbert, his craggy face turning white. 'Mankinder skins!'

'They're not skins,' squawked Paulie. 'They're football strips, although I must say they don't look much like the ones I saw on *Match of the Day.*'

'But what are they *for*?' Gina enquired, bending her long neck to get a better look at the jumble of shirts, shorts and socks.

'It's what footballers wear when they're playing a match,' Paulie explained. 'One team wears red, and the other blue,' he said, hopping over a pair of tattered red socks. 'And these are *shorts*,' he squawked, giving a pair of white shorts a peck with his sharp beak.

'This one's a different colour,' said Jengo, picking up a crumpled yellow top with a black collar.

'Ah, yes, that's the goalkeeper's shirt,' explained Paulie. 'Goalies always wear a different colour of top to the rest of the team.'

'What are we supposed to do with all this?' demanded Chaz, impatiently.

'You will *wear* them, of course,' replied Paulie. 'Each shirt has a different number on the back, and if we all wear the same colour, it shows that we are a team.'

'You must be joking!' exclaimed Herman. 'There's no way that shirt will fit me. It's far too small.'

'There are red strips and blue strips,' Becky said. 'Which ones should we wear?'

'I think we should wear red,' said Barney. 'That way you won't notice the blood if the Big Cats eat one of our players,' he shuddered.

Misha picked up a blue shirt. 'Meadow United should wear blue,' she said firmly. She began gathering up the blue shirts and handing them out to the players. 'Blue is the colour of the sky above our meadow and the lake from which we drink. It is the colour of butterflies and kingfishers, and the flowers that grow by the water's edge. Blue is the colour of the mountains first thing in the morning and of meadow grass in moonlight. So blue is the colour that Meadow United should wear.'

'Yes, blue!' chorused the animals.

And so, after a lot of huffing and puffing and stretching and squeezing into the shirts and shorts, the players lined up in front of Paulie dressed in the blue and white colours of Meadow United.

Obi and Misha stood side by side. The sleeves of their shirts were far too long and their shorts reached down to their feet. 'Now we're a proper team,' Misha whispered to Obi, 'and you are Meadow United's secret weapon.'

Obi looked at Misha and put on his bravest face. 'I'll try my best,' he said.

'I'm proud of you,' said Paulie, surveying his blue and white warriors. 'When the referee's whistle blows, Meadow United will be ready for those Big Cats!'

Suddenly, there was a loud tearing noise as Herman's shorts ripped. On the far side of the pitch, the orange and black striped monkeys began to sing.

Who ate all the pies?
Who ate all the pies?
You fat hippo, you fat hippo!
You ate all the pies!

Chapter 29
KICK OFF

The sun was low in the sky when the Big Cats arrived on the meadow.

Like an army, they marched towards the football pitch in perfect time. At the front was Boss, his long mane blowing in the breeze and his tail in the air. Behind him was the fearsome regiment of lions, cheetahs and leopards, with a cloud of red dust hovering in the air above them as they stamped across the ground.

Obi and the others watched in awe as the Big Cats approached. Behind Boss were Bex, Rio, Ralph, Anton and Tickles. Alongside the team jogged Mr Herbert, with a whistle round his neck. Then came the lionesses and other female cats, smaller, but no less frightening than the males. Bringing up the rear was the Big Cats supporters – more than a hundred lions, leopards and cheetahs, all chanting a menacing chorus:

We are The Big Cats!
We are The Big Cats!

At the same time, from the other direction, came the animals of the meadow. There were troops of monkeys, baboons, chimpanzees and gorillas, as well as herds of zebras, giraffes, wildebeests, warthogs and rhinos.

There were gangs of impalas, antelopes, rabbits and hedgehogs, and even a small procession of frogs and toads. Slowly they gathered around the football pitch, the smaller animals to the front and larger ones to the rear. As their numbers grew, the animals of the meadow began to sing.

Come on United!
Come on United!

By the time the sun dipped below the mpingo tree on top of the hill, a huge crowd was gathered around the pitch. The Big Cats supporters were behind one of the goals, while the animals of the meadow who outnumbered them were tightly packed round the other three sides of the pitch.

Then, as an enormous moon rose above the meadow and hung like a torch in the night sky, the two teams made their way onto the pitch. The Big Cats emerged like gladiators to the roar of their supporters and Boss took up his position on the touchline, growling instructions to his players.

Opposite them were the players of Meadow United, dressed in blue and white, with their supporters' cheers ringing loudly in their ears. Jengo took his place between the goalposts. In front of him, stood the defence – Barney and Becky the twin baboons, Gina and Engelbert. Ahead of them were Olive, Herman,

Walter and Zoe. In the centre circle with the ball at their feet and waiting to kick off, were Chaz and Obi.

Obi stared in dread at the Big Cats on the other side of the half way line. Close up they looked even bigger and more frightening than the first time they had visited the meadow. Anton, the fearsome leopard, was looking straight at him and licking his lips expectantly. Behind him, the lions, Rio, Tickles and Ralph, were pacing the turf menacingly, snarling and baring their huge fangs. Obi remembered the fate of poor Uncle Jeffrey, which made the hairs on his tail stand on end.

The most terrifying of all the Big Cats was Bex. The best footballer in the world stood on the halfway line sniffing the air, his eyes reflecting the moon like the headlights of a sports car. From his throat came a low, bloodcurdling growl. Obi's legs began to shake and he wanted to run away to the safety of the jungle. He turned to Chaz, hoping that his friend could provide some words of encouragement, when something caught his eye. Peeking out from underneath the white collar of the chimpanzee's football jersey was a pouch.

Obi rubbed his eyes. He thought he was seeing things, but there was no mistake - his leather pouch was hanging from the neck of his best friend. 'You stole that from me!' yelled Obi, staring at the pouch in dismay. 'You took it when I was asleep during that storm.'

'What, you mean *this*?' said Chaz innocently, pulling the pouch from under his collar.

Obi stared at the pouch. 'That's mine,' he yelled. 'Give it back to me!'

'I'll do no such thing,' said Chaz, indignantly. 'I found it lying on the meadow the other day. It's mine now and there is nothing you can do about it.'

'Please, Chaz!' begged Obi. 'I won't be any good at football unless I am wearing the Fact.'

Chaz tucked the pouch back under his shirt collar with a sly grin. 'Perhaps this lucky charm will work some magic for me,' he said, winking at Obi.

'But . . .'

'Shut up!' yelled the chimpanzee. 'The match is about to start. There's something else you need to know, Obi. I've decided that *I'm* going to be our team's striker, not you. Everyone knows that Chaz the chimpanzee strikes like lightening.'

'But what about our game plan?' cried Obi. 'Paulie said you were to be the target man.'

'Never mind what Paulie said,' hissed the chimpanzee. 'He's just a stupid parrot, pretending to know about football.' Chaz placed the ball on the centre spot and looked at Obi sternly. 'Chaz the chimpanzee is Meadow United's striker, and that's official.' He jabbed a finger into Obi's chest. 'You, on the other hand, are the dumbest monkey in the whole of Africa.'

Pheeeeep!

A sharp blast from Mr Herbert's whistle silenced the crowd and brought all the players to attention. The match was about to start. High above the meadow in the night sky, the stars flashed and glittered, and the moon cast long shadows across the pitch.

'Are both teams ready to begin the match?' the hyena asked.

'Ready!' roared the Big Cats.

'Ready!' cried the players of Meadow United.

'It's Meadow United to kick off,' Mr Herbert instructed. 'I want a nice fair game with no dirty tackles.'

'Come on United!' screeched Paulie, from his perch. 'Let's show them what we're made of. Let's give these Big Cats a match to remember.'

'Come on, Obi!' yelled Misha.

Pheeeeep!

And so, with a shrill blast from Mr Herbert's whistle and a roar from the crowd, the match began.

Meadow United versus the Big Cats.

Chapter 30

OWN GOAL

Chaz kicked off and passed the ball to Obi.

'*Come on Obi!*' yelled animals of the meadow, but the little monkey stood frozen to the spot. '*Pass the ball!*' roared the crowd, but Obi still didn't move. He stared goggle-eyed at the Big Cats, his knees knocking together and his heart racing, as they thundered towards him.

In the blink of an eye, Bex had whipped the ball from Obi's feet and was storming towards United's goal at full speed. Walter and Herman couldn't catch him, and Bex skipped over Engelbert's desperate tackle. '*Stop him! Stop the tiger!*' screeched Paulie, as Bex raced into the penalty area. But the Meadow United defenders couldn't stop Bex from unleashing a ferocious shot that flew past Jengo into the net.

Pheeeep!

GOAL! roared the Big Cats in the crowd. 'WHAT A GOAL!' They jumped up and down in celebration, slapping each other on the back and singing at the tops of their voices.

One-nil ... to the Cham-pions!
One-nil ... to the Cham-pions!
One-nil ... to the Cham-pions!
One-nil ... to the Cham-pions!

As the Big Cats players congratulated the tiger, Chaz turned angrily to Obi. 'What's the matter with you?' he yelled. 'The match has just started and we're already a goal down.' The chimpanzee's face was like thunder. 'It's your fault we lost that goal!'

Obi stared at the ground, wishing that a big hole would open up and swallow him. Chaz was right – the goal had been Obi's fault. Without the Fact round his neck, he'd completely forgotten how to play. Obi saw the disappointment on the faces of his team mates. One down already - what a terrible start to the match!

As both teams took up their positions for the restart, Boss prowled the touchline like a general inspecting his troops. 'Well done, boys,' he snarled. 'This is going to be even easier than I thought. These animals are hopeless at football.'

Chaz slammed the ball down on the centre spot and glowered at Obi. 'This time, you kick off to me,' he hissed, 'and I'll show you how it's done.'

Pheeeep! The referee's whistle sounded again and Obi stared at the ball. All he had to do was pass it to Chaz. Surely he could manage that!

Obi closed his eyes and stabbed his foot hopefully at the ball. Instead of going to Chaz, the ball sliced off Obi's foot and ended up at the paws of Anton the leopard who charged off at top speed towards the goal. As United's defenders rushed to tackle him, Anton skillfully flicked the ball to Zeff the cheetah, who gave it to Fang, the one-eyed lion.

'*Tackle them! Stop them!*' Paulie screeched, as Barney and Becky charged towards the lion from opposite sides. At the last moment, Fang stopped dead in his tracks and the twin baboons collided and tumbled to the ground. The one-eyed lion smashed the ball past Jengo and into the net.

Pheeeep!

GOAL! The Big Cats stood on their hind legs, punching the air and singing even more loudly.

One team has to go!
Has to leave the Meadow
United's team will have to go
They'll have to leave the meadow!

The animals of the meadow looked on, grim-faced and silent. The match had hardly begun and their team was already two goals down. Meadow United hadn't even managed to cross the halfway line.

Two minutes later, things got worse. Tickles the lion was about to shoot at the goal when Olive made a brave tackle and won the ball. Tickles collapsed to the ground as if he had been shot by a hunter's rifle. He rolled backwards and forwards on the ground, clutching a paw and howling in agony.

Boss raced onto the pitch, his face glowering. It

looked as if Boss might swallow Olive there and then. 'Foul, referee!' roared the lion. 'That ostrich is the dirtiest player I've ever seen. My players must be protected.'

Mr Herbert raced over. Pheeeep! Pheeeep! Pheeeep! Pheeeep! Pheeeep! 'That was the worst tackle I've ever seen,' the hyena barked at Olive. 'I wouldn't be surprised if you've broken this poor lion's leg.'

'But I won the ball fair and square,' protested Olive. 'I didn't touch him.'

'Off!' barked the hyena, waving a red card in Olive's face. As Olive walked off the pitch, the animals of the meadow looked even gloomier. On top of everything else, their team was now a player down.

'Free kick to the Big Cats!' Mr Herbert announced and Tickles suddenly made a remarkable recovery. Springing to his feet, the lion grabbed the ball and threw it to Bex, who was standing on his own near United's goal.

'Foul! Handball, referee!' the United players protested, but Mr Herbert shook his head. Bex thundered a shot with so much force that it whistled past Jengo and nearly burst the net.

Pheeeep!

GOAL! roared the Big Cats in the crowd. 'Three-nil!' The Big Cats hugged and kissed each other and danced with joy.

One Bex the Tiger!
There's only one Bex the Tiger!
One Bex the Ti-ger!
There's only one Bex the Ti-ger!

'Well done boys,' bellowed Boss. 'Three up already - this football match is as good as over. Meadow United are even worse than those Meerkats.'

The players of Meadow United trudged dejectedly back to their positions with their heads bowed. 'Come on, Obi!' yelled Misha from the touchline. 'Don't give up ... you can do it!'

Obi looked up and saw the worried faces of the meadow animal supporters who were standing round the pitch. Misha's right, he thought as Chaz kicked off again, we must score a goal. Taking a deep breath, he gathered the ball at his feet and crossed the halfway line. *'Go on, Obi!'* yelled United's supporters; their spirits lifted at the sight of a Meadow United player moving into the Big Cats half.

But before Obi could get any further, the fearsome lion called Scarface appeared and with one ferocious swing of his back leg, he kicked the little monkey high into the night sky.

'That's got to be a foul, referee!' screeched Paulie, as Obi somersaulted through the air.

'Play on!' cried Mr Herbert, shaking his head. 'Perfectly fair tackle - the monkey dived!'

The ball broke to Zeff the cheetah, who crossed it into United's penalty area. Anton reached the ball before Gina and stabbed it past Jengo into the back of net.

Pheeeep!

'Four-nil!' roared the Big Cats, dancing a jig and singing even more loudly.

Are you Meerkats!
Are you Meerkats!
Are you Meerkats in disguise?
Are you Meerkats in disguise?

And just when it seemed things couldn't get any worse, it was 5-0. From a Big Cats corner kick, the ball bounced towards Obi. *'Run, Obi … run!'* yelled the crowd, but when Obi felt the snarling presence of Scarface looming up behind him he panicked and closed his eyes, kicking the ball away as hard as he could. When he opened his eyes, Obi watched in horror as the ball sailed over the heads of United's defenders and into the net.

Meadow United had scored at last, but it was an *own goal!* What a disaster.

As the Big Cats supporters hooted with laughter, Obi sunk to his knees in despair and held his head in his hands.

Who put the ball in United's net!
Monkey ... Monkey!
Who put the ball in United's net!
That stupid Monkey did!
Stupid Monkey did!
Stupid Monkey did!
Who put the ball in United's net!
That stupid Monkey did!

When Mr Herbert's whistle blew for half time, the Meadow United players left the pitch with the chants of the Big Cats army ringing in their ears.

Easy! .... Easy! .... Easy! .... Easy!

Chapter 31
HEARING THINGS

'What was that noise?'

The film crew stopped, their faces lit up by the glare of their torches.

'I heard it too,' whispered the cameraman.

'Sounded like a lion,' said the sound engineer.

They stood for a while, listening carefully in the darkness of the jungle. 'It's been a long day,' said the director. 'Maybe we're starting to hear things.'

'Wait, there it is again!' cried the cameraman. 'I definitely heard something that time!'

'What do you think it is?' asked the engineer, gripping his machete more tightly.

'Can't be lions,' said the director. 'Not here, in the middle of the jungle.'

'Definitely a big cat,' insisted the cameraman. 'What do you think, Emily?'

Emily Jackson shone the torch at her grandfather's map. 'I think we're getting close,' she whispered.

'Look! Over there!' cried the engineer, pointing into the distance where bright moonlight shone through a gap in the trees.

Chapter 32

HALF TIME

The players sat round the charred remains of Engelbert's tree. It was half time and Meadow United were losing by five goals to nil. The players stared at the ground in disbelief.

'The match is as good as over,' grunted Herman, breaking the silence. 'We're lucky to be only five goals down – it could easily have been ten!'

'All I did in the first half was pick the ball out of our net,' said Jengo, shaking his head in dismay.

'We didn't manage a single shot at the Big Cats goal,' said Becky.

'The Big Cats are too fast,' said Gina.

'And the referee is against us too,' said Zoe. 'He sent Olive off for a perfectly fair tackle.'

Chaz jumped to his feet. 'Don't blame the referee, it's *his* fault that we're losing,' he shouted, pointing an accusing finger at Obi. 'Get the ball to Obi he'll score the goals,' he added, sarcastically. 'Whenever Obi gets the ball, we end up *losing* a goal!' Chaz crossed his arms and stared grimly at Obi. 'And you even managed to score against your own team. It's unbelievable!'

Obi's eyes filled with tears. 'I know,' he said, in a small voice. 'I've let the team down badly.'

'So much for being our secret weapon,' sneered Chaz. 'We'd stand a better chance if you were playing for the Big Cats instead of us.'

'Obi was just unlucky,' panted Engelbert, trying to get his breath back. 'He was doing his best; we all were. I'm afraid the Big Cats are just too good for us.'

Wiping away a tear, Obi looked at Chaz, who had once been his best friend, someone he'd looked up to and admired. He noticed the leather pouch under the collar of Chaz's shirt. 'The Fact hasn't brought you much luck after all,' he said, softly.

'I haven't a clue what you're talking about,' Chaz snorted, turning his back on Obi.

Misha looked up at Paulie. 'What about the second half, Paulie? What should do?'

Paulie surveyed his battered and bruised team. Their heads were down and they looked like they had given up. Engelbert was gasping for breath and the twin baboons had huge bruises on their heads. Walter's shirt was ripped and there were claw marks on the warthog's back where Scarface had jumped on him. Gina was limping badly and Herman could hardly see, because a Big Cat had jabbed a sharp claw into his eyes.

Paulie took a deep breath and spoke to his players. 'What can I say,' he croaked. 'The second half is about to begin and we are five goals behind. It looks as if we are down and out, but I know we can fight our way back into this match, if we believe in each other, if we play with our hearts.

'But, I'm just an old parrot and I can't do it for you. You have to look at the players standing next to you and know that they are ready to sacrifice themselves for this team because they know you'll do the same.

'You have to play with your hearts, but you also need to have fire in your belly! You must go and play the second half as if it is the last game you'll ever play. You have to look your team mates in the eye and let them know that you'll give everything you have in the battle for our meadow. That's what makes the difference between winning and losing . . . between living and dying!'

Paulie cast his eyes over the players of Meadow United. 'Will do that?' he said softly.

Obi jumped to his feet. 'I will!' he cried.

One by one the other animals stood up. 'I will!' Engelbert roared, his trunk curled high in the air.

'We will!' cried Barney and Becky, slapping each other on the back.

'Let's get back out there and teach those Big Cats a lesson,' yelled Gina.

Herman beat his hooves on the ground and Jengo thumped his chest with his huge fists. Paulie saw a new determination on the faces of his players. He saw hope swelling in their hearts and fire in their bellies.

With Obi leading the way, the players of Meadow United marched back onto the pitch.

Chapter 33
THEY THINK IT'S ALL OVER

Obi stood on the half way line, waiting for the second half to begin. He watched the Big Cats swagger back onto the pitch - Rio, Anton, Scarface, Ralph, Bex and the others – with arrogant grins on their faces. Boss was prowling the touchline, winking at his players and saying, 'Go on boys ... finish them off!'

They think it's all over, thought Obi, as he watched the Big Cats take up their positions. He looked at the meadow animals packed around the pitch, all hoping that Meadow United would somehow save them from a terrible fate.

Mr Herbert put the whistle to his lips. 'Are both teams ready?' barked the hyena.

'Ready!' roared the Big Cats.

'Ready!' cried Meadow United.

Pheeeeep!

Bex kicked off, but before the ball reached one of the Big Cats, Obi moved like a phantom to spirit the ball away. He raced deep into the Big Cats half, skipping over tackles, his blue shirt flapping like a sail. Suddenly, Scarface appeared in front of him, snarling fiercely. Obi closed his eyes, waiting for the lion to kick him into the air again, but just then he heard Misha's words.

'It wasn't the Fact, Obi,
It was you!'

As Scarface rushed towards him, Obi ducked and darted between the lion's legs. He found himself on the edge of the Big Cats penalty box and kicked the football as hard as he could. The ball flew like a rocket, and Obi watched in amazement as it sped past the Big Cats keeper into the net.

Pheeeep!

GOAL!

At last Meadow United's supporters had something to cheer about. *'Come on United!'* they cried and sang a song of their own.

Who put the ball in The Big Cats net?
Obi ... Obi!
Who put the ball in The Big Cats net?
Obi the Monkey did!

'Sssssssensssssational ssssstrike,' hissed Sigmund the snake, who had appeared at the edge of the pitch along with Carl the crocodile.

'Our little monkey friend nearly burst the net with that shot,' observed Carl.

And it wasn't long before United scored a second goal. Herman won a tackle on the halfway line and passed the ball to Obi, who dribbled past five astonished Big Cats players.

'Stop him!' Boss commanded, from the touchline, 'Stop that monkey!'

But there was no stopping Obi as he left the last defender in his wake and lobbed the ball skillfully over the Big Cats goalkeeper into the net.

Pheeeep!

GOAL! yelled the animals of the meadow, hailing their team's unexpected fight back. They whooped and cheered and hugged each other. Now it was five goals to two, and United were back in the match! This time it was the Big Cats army that were silent as United's supporters sang even more loudly.

You're not singing!
You're not singing!
You're not singing any more!
You're not singing any more!

Play continued furiously from one end of the pitch to the other. The animals were so engrossed in the match that none of them noticed Emily and the film crew emerging from the jungle. They were astonished at what they saw.

What on earth is happening? Emily wondered. *What is this place? Was she dreaming?*

'Unless my eyes are deceiving me,' gasped the sound engineer, 'there appears to be a . . . a . . . football match going on!'

'I must be going mad!' whispered the cameraman. 'I can see animals wearing football strips!'

'Look at those big cats!' cried the director, his eyes nearly popping out of his head. 'I'm sure I can see a *tiger* playing football!'

'Impossible! There aren't tigers in Africa!'

'And look at all these animals around the pitch!' yelled the cameraman. 'There must be thousands of them watching the match. It's incredible!'

Emily ran towards the action. 'Quick, start filming!' she yelled. 'I don't know what's going on here, but if we don't get this on film nobody's going to believe us.'

They watched in amazement as a warthog wearing a blue and white football strip thundered past them with the ball. The warthog passed to a hippopotamus, who gave it to a zebra, who flicked it to a monkey, who thrashed it past a lion into the net.

GOAL! roared the crowd as Obi's shot hit the net. The noise shook the meadow like an explosion and the film crew looked on in astonishment as the animals around them danced for joy! It was five goals to three, and United's supporters were singing loudly.

We shall not . . . we shall not be moved!
We shall not . . . we shall not be moved!
Not by the lions, the leopards or the tigers!
We shall not be moved!

'Great goal Obi!' screeched Paulie. 'Come on United, we're only two goals behind now. You can do it!'

On the opposite side of the pitch, with his face like thunder, Boss bellowed orders at the Big Cats. 'Stop him!' roared the lion, pounding his massive paw on the ground. 'I am ordering you to stop that monkey!'

But Obi was too quick for the Big Cats. He dribbled the ball so skillfully that he was past them in the blink of an eye. He danced through their tackles like a ghost, skipping over their desperate attempts to chop, slash and scythe him down. 'Go on Obi!' yelled the crowd, as he weaved his way once more past the lions and leopards.

As the moon rose high in the night sky and a million stars twinkled and glistened, Meadow United fought their way back. Barney and Becky tackled like demons, while Gina and Engelbert cleared the ball time after time. Walter and Herman won tackles in midfield, while Zoe fired dangerous crosses into the Big Cats penalty area. At the other end of the pitch, Jengo made a fantastic save as Bex took another powerful shot at United's goal.

'Are you getting this?' the director whispered to the cameraman.

'Yes, yes!' cried the cameraman. 'Just wait until this goes on TV. Never mind those missing miners, this football match is going to be the news story of the century!'

'Look, the blue team are bringing on a substitute,' said the sound engineer. 'They're taking off the chimpanzee.'

'That's no surprise,' said the director. 'The chimpanzee was the worst player on the pitch.'

Chaz shook his head in disbelief. 'What? You're substituting *me*?' he yelled angrily at Paulie. 'Are you crazy? I'm the team's star player.'

'We need a fresh player and there isn't much time left,' Paulie yelled. 'Misha will take your place in attack.'

'That's not fair!' yelled Chaz, storming off the pitch. He took off his shirt and threw it down on the ground. 'You're replacing *me* with ... with ... a useless monkey!' he screamed, shaking with rage. 'Now we'll definitely lose the match, and it'll be your fault!'

As Chaz left the pitch, he tore the pouch from his neck and flung it into the night.

'Corner to the blue team,' announced the sound engineer, pointing to the far side of the pitch. 'This is exciting.'

Obi placed the ball beside the corner flag. He took two steps back and then waited for his team mates to reach the Big Cats penalty area. We need to score, Obi said to himself. We're running out of time. Taking a deep breath, Obi stepped forward and fired the corner kick into the box.

The lions jumped and the leopards leapt and the cheetahs sprung into the air, but none of them reached the ball because jumping highest in the night sky was a wrinkled old elephant. Obi watched in amazement as Engelbert crashed a powerful header into the net.

GOAL! roared the crowd, as United's players rushed to congratulate Engelbert. 'Who says an elephant can't jump!' wheezed Engelbert, with an enormous grin on his craggy face.

'Come on!' yelled Obi, clapping his hands and urging his players on. 'It's five-four . . . we still have time for an equaliser.'

The meadow grew darker as the moon disappeared behind a cloud. There were worried looks on the Big Cats faces as they lined up for the restart. They looked nervously at their manager for instructions. 'What should we do, Boss?' asked Tickles the lion.

'Keep the ball away from that monkey, whatever you do,' demanded Boss. 'We're still one goal up and there isn't much time left.'

But there was no stopping Meadow United. If they were going to lose the match, they were going to go down fighting. Avoiding the lunging tackles of the Big Cats defenders, Becky charged up the wing and crossed the ball to Obi, who fired a shot high into the Big Cats net.

GOAL! yelled the crowd, as the players raced back to their positions. Now it was five goals each. Meadow

United had fought their way back from the jaws of defeat.

'What an incredible match,' cried the engineer. 'How on earth did these animals learn to play football?'

With the full-time whistle rapidly approaching, there was still time for one of the teams to score a winner. Suddenly Bex got the ball and, with his yellow eyes gleaming, the tiger stormed towards United's goal, brushing off tackles and leaving blue-shirted defenders trailing in his wake.

'Oh, no!' screeched Paulie, covering his eyes with his wings as the tiger raced into the penalty area. Just as the world's best player prepared to score the winning goal, Gina the giraffe appeared from nowhere, stretching out a long leg and clearing the ball to safety. Bex catapulted through the air with his legs stretched out in all directions. As the flailing tiger crashed to the ground, the Big Cats turned to the referee.

Chapter 34

QUICK AS A FLASH

The crowd held its breath as Mr Herbert raced towards United's penalty area.

'I don't believe it!' snapped Carl. 'The referee is going to give a penalty.'

'Never a penalty!' hissed Sigmund. 'It was a dive if ever I saw one.'

The crowd held its breath as Mr Herbert put the whistle to his lips. If the Big Cats got a penalty, Bex would surely smash one of his cannonball shots into the back of the net and the Big Cats would win the match. Then the meadow would belong to them.

Just then, the moon reappeared from behind the clouds and lit up a patch of ground where Emily stood. Something caught her eye. It was an old leather pouch.

'Blow your whistle, referee!' screamed Boss. 'What are you waiting for? It's a penalty!'

Emily could feel something heavy inside the pouch. She loosened the ties and took out the African Queen. She gasped as the meadow was filled with the colours of the rainbow and the lights of a thousand dancing stars. The explosion of light that illuminated the pitch seemed to hold Mr Herbert and the players in a spell.

Only one player wasn't affected. Quick as a flash, Obi got the ball and ran as fast as he could towards the Big Cats empty goal. There wasn't a single player standing in his way.

But as Obi crossed the halfway line, the spell was broken and all the other players realised what was happening. With a blood-curdling roar, the Big Cats set off in pursuit of him. Obi ran and ran but he could hear the Big Cats coming up fast behind him, roaring and snarling furiously.

'Go on, Obi!' yelled the crowd.

'Stop him!' roared Boss.

'Look at that monkey go!' cried the director.

'You can do it!' shouted Emily. 'Keep going little monkey, you can do it . . .'

Chapter 35
GOLDEN GOAL

Obi was running as fast as his legs would carry him, but it's a well-known fact that a cheetah has a top speed of 70 miles per hour, which is much faster than even the quickest monkey. Just as Obi was about to kick the ball into the net, one of the cheetahs caught up with him and tore its sharp claws into Obi's blue shirt, sending the monkey tumbling to the ground. From every direction, lions, tigers, leopards and cheetahs charged towards the ball, but another monkey got there before any of the Big Cats. Obi opened his eyes just in time to see Misha shoot the ball into the Big Cats net.

For a moment, the meadow was silent. The crowd, the players and the film crew were stunned and stood quite still, as if captured in a photograph. Then, a shrill blast of the referee's whistle shattered the silence and brought the meadow back to life.

Pheeeeeep!

GOAL! cried all the animals of the meadow. *GOAL! GOAL! GOAL!*

As Meadow United's players jumped for joy, the animals of the meadow raced onto the pitch to celebrate their team's victory. Baboons and gorillas hugged each other, zebras danced victory jigs with warthogs, rhinos sank to their knees and kissed the dusty ground, while monkeys and chimpanzees leapt up and down and waved their arms in the air. Meadow United had done it! They had beaten the Big Cats by six goals to five in the most amazing football match ever played.

Suddenly an enormous roar interrupted the celebrations and Obi turned to see a furious lion racing towards him.

Chapter 36
A BLUE AND WHITE WALL

'Make a fool of me, would you?' roared Boss, as he thundered across the pitch towards Obi. 'I should have got rid of you when I had the chance.'

'Run Obi!' yelled Misha.

As Boss closed in on Obi, the little monkey took off and scampered across the meadow.

'You'll never outrun me,' snarled Boss, baring his sharp fangs as he continued after Obi. 'And when I'm finished with you, I'll be back for your friends.'

But suddenly, Boss found himself up against a blue and white wall. The players of Meadow United stood in front of him, shoulder to shoulder, making it impossible for him to chase after Obi.

'Out of my way!' roared Boss. 'I have a dinner engagement with a monkey.'

The animals didn't move. 'You promised you'd leave us in peace if Meadow United won the match,' said Engelbert. 'So it's time for you and the Big Cats to leave our meadow.'

'You fools!' roared the lion. 'Did you really think we were going to let you leave this meadow? Don't you know what Big Cats eat?'

More animals of the meadow joined the wall of players standing in front of Boss.

'Chimpanzees, giraffes, warthogs and zebras -

there's enough food on this meadow to last the Big Cats a whole season,' roared Boss. 'And I'm going to start with that insolent monkey, so out of my way!'

'You'll have to get past us first!' cried Herman.

'You won't stop me,' roared Boss, standing nose to nose with the animals. The lion took several paces back and then sprinted forward, leaping over Misha's head and setting off again at full speed.

'Run Obi!' Misha screamed again.

Obi was running like the wind, but a lion is much faster than a monkey and as Obi began to tire, he glanced over his shoulder to see the snarling lion gaining on him. I'm not going to make it, Obi thought, as he raced across the moonlit meadow. I'm never going to see my friends again.

Obi reached the hill just a few seconds ahead of Boss and began climbing the purple rocks, hoping that he would be safe at the top. To his horror Obi saw that the lion was clambering up the hill after him.

On the meadow below, the animals and film crew were watching their every move. 'The monkey's got no chance,' the director whispered to Emily. 'Even if he makes it to the top, he's got nowhere to go.'

Obi clambered over the last few rocks and ran across some planks of wood. Now he was at the top of the hill and behind him was the cliff edge, with a sheer drop to the meadow below. Moments later the fearsome face of Boss appeared, his mane blowing in the meadow breeze.

'Say goodbye to your meadow,' grinned Boss, licking his lips as he closed in on Obi. Suddenly there was a loud snap as the wood gave way under the weight of the huge lion. Boss began to lose his balance as first one plank, then another, broke and fell into the mineshaft below. Obi saw the expression on the lion's face change from a grin to a look of fear as he balanced precariously on the last remaining plank, the moon reflected in his eyes like small gold coins.

'Help me!' commanded Boss, but it was too late - the last plank of wood splintered, then snapped and, before he could say anything else, the lion disappeared into the mineshaft.

On the meadow below, the defeated army of Big Cats turned and began their slow march home. Emily Jackson stood smiling in the centre circle of the football pitch with the African Queen held high, sparkling and glittering, and lighting up the meadow like a magical fireworks display.

Chapter 37
THE HERO

Obi was sitting on his favourite rock. It was another hot day and the meadow was still and peaceful, apart from the occasional squawk of a parrot in the jungle. On the dusty red ground below, Chaz was counting bananas and placing them in a large pile.

'Twenty-eight . . . twenty-nine . . . thirty. Here's thirty bananas for your breakfast, just like I promised. Would you like me to peel one for you?' asked Chaz, eagerly. 'Or maybe I could chop them into little pieces to make it easier for you to eat?'

'That would be nice, thanks,' laughed Obi, although there's no way I'll ever eat thirty bananas.'

On the meadow below, Obi could hear Engelbert, Paulie, Misha, Gina and all his friends reliving the previous night's football match - recalling every pass, tackle, shot, and goal. He chuckled as he saw Engelbert jump into the air to head an imaginary ball, demonstrating his famous goal to an audience of impressed young monkeys.

'Shall I could collect some palm nuts for you?' suggested Chaz, helpfully. 'Or maybe some juicy berries?'

'These bananas will do nicely, thank you,' said Obi, thinking about the events of the previous night. Meadow United had won a fantastic victory and the defeated Big Cats were gone forever.

'I hope you haven't forgotten about my football lesson after breakfast?' said Chaz, anxiously.

'No, I haven't forgotten,' said Obi. It was interesting how much more friendly Chaz had become towards him. Nothing was too much trouble for the chimpanzee.

'Are you comfortable?' Chaz asked. 'Would you like me to get you something to sit on?'

Obi gazed down upon the meadow. In the distance he could see the strange mankinders climbing the hill. He noticed that the one with long dark hair was wearing the pouch round her neck.

'What an amazing place,' said Emily, taking in the beauty of the meadow, the lake and the distant mountains.

'This must have been the diamond mine,' said the cameraman peering down into the mineshaft. 'Looks like it goes down a long way.'

'Careful,' warned Emily, 'You don't want to end up like that lion.'

'I've found some old tools,' said the sound engineer, shaking the dust off a rusty shovel.

'Seems the legend might have been true after all,' said the director.

'What will you do with it, Emily?' asked the cameraman. 'The diamond, I mean.'

A cool breeze passed across the meadow, whistling

gently through the long grass and stirring the leaves of the acacia trees. Emily closed her eyes and, for the briefest moment, she thought she could hear distant voices echoing across the meadow.

African Queen ... African Queen!
The biggest diamond there's ever been!

'Did you hear that?' Emily said.

'Hear what?' asked the director.

'Voices,' said Emily, closing her eyes again. 'Can't you hear them?'

Good shot Stanley!
Penalty!
One nil to the Reds!

'I can't hear anything,' said the sound engineer, shaking his head. 'Apart from some parrots squawking.'

When Emily opened her eyes, the voices had gone.

'I wonder what happened to the miners,' said the cameraman.

'I don't think we'll ever know,' said the sound engineer. 'Guess it'll always be a mystery.'

'Time to go home,' said the director, lifting his backpack. 'We've a long journey ahead of us.'

While the film crew made its way down the hill,

Emily remained at the top, peering into the mineshaft. Loosening the ties of the leather pouch, she removed the diamond and held it in her hand for a moment, taking in its sparkle and deep flashes of colour.

'I guess this is where you belong,' she whispered, and she dropped the African Queen into the blackness of the mineshaft. Without looking back, Emily climbed down the hill and joined the film crew on the meadow.

From his favourite rock, Obi watched the mankinders disappear through a gap in the trees and into the jungle.

'What a beautiful day,' said Misha, who had joined Obi and Chaz on the rock.

Moments later, in a flurry of grey feathers, Paulie landed next to them. 'How does the hero of Meadow United feel this morning?' squawked Paulie. I don't suppose you got much sleep last night.'

Obi laughed as he remembered how the celebrations had continued long into the night, until the first rays of morning sun bathed the meadow in a warm glow. 'I'm not a hero,' he said, modestly. 'It was your team talk that made us believe in ourselves. If anyone's a hero Paulie, it's you!'

'It was a wonderful speech,' Misha agreed. 'How did you know what to say to the team at half time?'

Paulie cocked his head to one side. 'I think I heard it on TV,' he squawked. 'African grey parrots are very good at copying what mankinders say, you know.'

Obi gazed at the animals grazing peacefully on the meadow below. The meadow had never felt more like home than it did on this beautiful sunny morning and it was where they belonged.

'Come on guys!' he cried, climbing down the rock. 'Anyone fancy a game of football?

'If I've said it once, I've said it a hundred times,' yelled Chaz, scampering down behind him, 'monkeys are the *best* footballers in the world.'

'And that ... is a fact!'

*   *   *   *   *   *